Ro

WHEN APPS
BITE BACK,
ONLY SCIENCE
CAN SAVE
THE DAY

HOOOOO
WWWLLL!

MEET THE
CHARACTERS

Tyler:
An all-round Einstein-obsessed genius.
- Natural leader
- Photographic memory
- Not a fan of the outdoors

Ashley:
An ingenious inventor, she can turn
any collection of junk into something useful.
- Straight-talking
- Allergic to dogs
- Always carries a screwdriver

Dylan:
Expert hacker with an extraordinary IQ.
- Loves candy
- Adores algorithms
- Adorable . . . kind of like a puppy.

Kipper & Pipper:
Camp leaders and 'Big Squirrels'
- Love to sing
- Not fans of phones or books
- Obsessed with aromatherapy

Peggy & Herbert:
Experts on how to survive camp!
- Woodlice
- Planning an escape
- Can be trusted in a crisis

Courtney:
A mean girl!
- Chief cheerleader
- Expert baton twirler
- All-round nerd tormentor

OXFORD
UNIVERSITY PRESS

Great Clarendon Street, Oxford OX2 6DP
Oxford University Press is a department of the University of Oxford.
It furthers the University's objective of excellence in research, scholarship,
and education by publishing worldwide. Oxford is a registered trade mark
of Oxford University Press in the UK and in certain other countries

British Library Cataloguing in Publication Data

Data available

ISBN: 978-0-19-276691-5

1 3 5 7 9 10 8 6 4 2

Printed in Great Britain

Paper used in the production of this book is a natural,
recyclable product made from wood grown in sustainable forests.
The manufacturing process conforms to the environmental
regulations of the country of origin.

Graph paper: Alfonso de Tomas/Shutterstock.com

Tom McLaughlin

YOU'VE BEEN WERE-WOLFED

OXFORD
UNIVERSITY PRESS

BEGONE NERDLINGS BEGONE

For me, the summer is something that happens
to other people. I just don't get it. As soon as
there's a hint of sunshine everyone spends
all day trying to slow-roast themselves like a
freaky BBQ. Summer is when all the most bitey
creatures come out, and when all the most
skin-scratchy plants come into bloom. Mother
Nature is giving us a clear sign—stay indoors!
Get off the beaches, step away from the seas,

and please keep out of my forests, you just don't belong here. The great outdoors for me just grates. My dad was always trying to take me camping when I was younger. Imagine going somewhere on holiday and having to build your own house when you get there. I have one rule when it comes to holidays: you should never go anywhere worse than where you live. That's why I've decided to spend this summer at home, working on my own projects, indoors, away from all the heat and violence. I have a hologram phone that I'm building, plus some bacterial growth that I'm really excited about. An entire summer away from this dumb school and the useless teachers, just me, my books, and my friends, Ashley and Dylan, and when the bell goes in 3 minutes, I'll be free.

'Tyler, are you listening to me?'

'Yes!' I snap myself out of my daydream. 'The answer is x to the power of y minus the square root!' I blurt out, suddenly remembering that I'm in class.

'That's all very well, Tyler, but this is English. We're talking about myths and legends, you know like seriously spooky stuff. Tell me, do you know how to spot or even kill a werewolf—this is important stuff!' Mr Jones says, looking at me really seriously. Mr Jones is the head teacher of our school. He is a former model and hopelessly in love with himself. He's so far the only man I have ever seen trying to rock a three-piece denim suit.

'Erm, no,' I reply, 'but I don't think it's ever going to come up. I mean, these aren't real creatures,' I tell him calmly. There are gasps from the rest of the class.

'These are *real* legends, Tyler,' Mr Jones snaps. 'You best pay attention. This stuff could save your life one day.' He continues with the

lesson: 'You can spot a werewolf by the wild look in its eyes, and the way its nose twitches and quivers. Any other clues people?'

'They also look like a dog?' Blane yells out.

'Yes!' Mr Jones snaps. 'They also look like a dog. They say the ears are the first to appear, then the tail and claws, although I've never seen one myself,' Mr Jones shrugs.

'Yes,' I say, 'but you're talking about legends. Of course you haven't seen one, no one has because they aren't real, them being legends and all that.' I look around, waiting for the rest of the class to back me up.

'Not true, Tyler!' a boy called Brody chips in. 'I was watching the news and there was this story about boy who was stuck in a park with loads of monsters in.'

'That wasn't the news, that was *Jurassic Park*. You were probably watching Netflix you jam head,' I blurt out.

'Just because you can't see it, doesn't mean it's not there. I can't see air, but apparently that's real,' Mr Jones says wisely.

'Glass!' another person shouts out. 'You can't see glass, but that's real. If it wasn't all my juice would just spill.'

'What?' I say. I'm just about to argue the difference between glass and werewolves when I get hit with an avalanche of other things you can't see.

'Water!'

'Clingfilm!'

'The invisible man—how do we know he's not real?' Someone shouts out.

'What are you all talking about?!' I try to reason with them but I'm completely drowned out.

'All we are saying, Fitz,' Mr Jones adds, 'is that just because it may not be real to you, doesn't mean it's not real to other people. Facts are opinions.' He smiles smugly.

'No, facts are facts, opinions are quite different!' I try to get out, but it's too late, the bell goes. A huge cheer goes up across the school, like a champagne bottle of human happiness has just been popped.

'Surely you can see that I'm right?' I say to Mr Jones.

'Who cares,' he beams. 'I'm out of here, see you losers in September!' he yells, before doing the shape of an 'L' on his forehead and jumping out of the half-opened window and into his car. He's clearly been planning his escape for some time—there's a suitcase on the roof and the engine's running. I hear a squeal of rubber and then he's gone in a puff of smoke.

'But what about Big Foot's shoe size!' Brody bellows after him.

'I guess some things are meant to remain a mystery,' I smile at Brody and head out of class. This is the best day since I moved to this place with my dad. Happyville, according to scientific fact, and by scientific fact I mean someone in a white coat making stuff up, is the 'happiest town in the world'. Let me paint a picture for you. Imagine a clothes shop filled with smiling mannequins wearing bright clothes. They all have happy faces and big plastic hair. Now imagine if all those dummies came to life and made your life hell. Now you have a pretty good idea of what this place is like. If it wasn't for my two friends, Ashley and Dylan, I'd be in real trouble. They're misfits like me. I'm Tyler Fitz by the way, but you can call me Fitz. I know, I'm aware of the coincidence— Miss Fitz by name and by nature. Don't get me wrong, I like the idea of a school where you actually learn stuff, but last week we had to write an essay on why puppies are aces.

I file out of the classroom door and into the corridor. It feels like I'm being released from prison.

'Hey Fitz!' Ashley yells to me from down the corridor.

'Hey Ash! We're free!' I grin.

'Freedom is just an illusion, Fitz. You know that, aimed at keeping the masses down.' Ashley can be a little bit serious, but she is one hell of an inventor, so you have to take the rough with the smooth. 'What are your plans for the summer?' she asks.

'I'm making a hologram phone,' I reply. 'I've just about got the prototype going. I still need to stabilize the display but I'm getting there. And for those days when I just want to kick back and relax, I've got a new volume of algebraic equations to crack open. Do you want join me?'

'Wow, sure. I'm pretty busy harvesting my family's DNA in an attempt to build an army of replicas, but I'll definitely help when I can.'

'Does your family have any idea you're planning on replacing them with clones?' I ask.

'Nah,' Ashley replies with a cool stare.

'Would it not be easier to clone a pet?'

'Nope, I'm allergic to almost all animals. There's one variety of parasitic wasp that I'm able to tolerate, but the pet store just looked at me weird when I went in to enquire about buying a nest. Anything else just makes me all sneezy and blotchy,' Ashley shrugs.

'What are you going to do with the originals?' I say, returning to the subject of her cloning her family.

'I'm thinking about selling Subject One on eBay.' Subject One is what Ashley calls her Mum. 'I want to see if I get any interest. If it works I might sell the rest on there too. I'm hoping to raise some money for a new batch of uranium, but we'll see—the UN are starting to get nosey. Maybe I could swap. Is there a place where you can go to swap your parents for nuclear material?'

'I think it might be called jail, Ashley.'

'Hey, you guys! School's out for

su-u-u-u-u-ummer!' Dylan sings as she comes crashing into us both, strumming an imaginary guitar. 'Those are the lyrics to a pop song I heard on the radio three months ago, and I've been waiting to sing them ever since then. It wasn't my radio of course, I don't have anything that cool in my bedroom. I'm not into pop music or anything with fast rhythms. They make my braces rattle and brain fizz,' Dylan explains, in her nerdy, puppy dog way.

'We're talking about our plans for the summer. What are you up to?' I ask.

'I get to spend the whole summer working on my new video game. Imagine chess, it's in seven dimensions, and has unicorns.'

'Cool,' I say. 'Do you want to come round

13

mine for a bite to eat? We could hang out in the den for a bit, maybe crack open a couple of algebra books for a laugh?' I say.

'When you say "bite to eat" . . .?' Ashley looks at me nervously.

'Don't worry, it'll be bland and boiled,' I reassure her, remembering how many things she's allergic to.

'OK, I'm in,' Ashley says, considering the offer for a moment. 'Just keep me away from all those exotic spices your dad likes to throw around like confetti at a family wedding.'

'It was salt and pepper, Ashley,' I smile. 'But I take your point.' We head out into the daylight to grab our scooters.

'Well I must say, I'm going to enjoy not

being around you three
brain drains this summer,'
a familiar voice pipes up.
We turn round and there
she is. Batman has the Joker,
and I have Courtney: Chief
Cheerleader, Homecoming Queen and all-round
Nerd Tormentor, she is two years above me
and therefore thinks I'm some sort of pet.

'What are you doing this summer?
Probably inventing a new colour, or learning all
the numbers, or something equally stupid,' she
hisses.

'That's right, we're going to learn all the
numbers,' I sigh, playing along. 'We'll probably
start with the highest and work backwards.'

'Duh, everyone knows it's a million,' Courtney scoffs. Ashley scowls back, while Dylan pretends she's looking at her shoes. 'Well just as long as you stay away from me. I'm off to Happyville Summer Camp, to like, totally get in touch with nature and get some rest after a long season of cheerleading. But that's probably something you wouldn't be able to cope with. I know how you feel about insects, Dylan.'

'I don't trust anything with more legs than me,' Dylan says, not making eye contact.

'I'm not listening. Don't ever assume that I'm listening to you. Begone nerdlings, begone . . . !' she says, wafting us away like she's shooing a chicken.

'I don't think she likes us,' Dylan shrugs, as we grab our scooters and head home. As we glide along the streets we go past scores of people washing their cars and mowing their lawns. The more I get to know this place the more I feel like a stranger. It's like living in a holiday brochure—everything's beautiful but empty. But even this strange town is not going

to put me in a bad mood. Nothing will. I have my friends, I am free, and we have six weeks of doing our own thing. If this was a musical this would be the point where everyone starts singing and dancing to a number with plinky plonk piano sounds and a heart-tugging chord change or two.

))))

'Peachy Pie, is that you?' We come in through the front door and I can hear the sound of my Dad at his old typewriter. He's thumping away at his novel, the thing that we moved here in the first place for, so that Dad would have time to think, grow vegetables, and write his definitive work.

'Hey Dad, the girls are here,' I shout back.

'How's the book going?'

'Good news!' he yells from the study. 'I think I've come up with a title. How does "The Book of Words" sound!' he yells excitedly.

'Well, there's no doubting what it is,' I tell him helpfully. 'It's a good start. Maybe you can spend next week thinking of the first chapter title?' I say encouragingly.

'Whoa, slow down, I don't think I'm finished working on the title yet. I'm not sure about the first word—it sounds too needy,' he says, scrutinizing the paper.

'You think "the" sounds too needy?'

'What's the book about, Brian?' Ashley asks.

'Well, it's like the future, and you're in the

past and I think there might be a robot, or it could be a wizard, and then it all flips around,' Dad begins to explain.

'In other words, he doesn't know,' I whisper to the girls. 'Also it's weird that you call my Dad by his first name.'

'I'm trying to be polite. Isn't that what other humans do?' Ashley asks. 'Brian's all right with it, aren't you, Brian?' Ashley says, looking confused. She's not a girl who understands social rules.

'Oh never mind. Now, who's for three glasses of refreshing water?' I offer.

'OK, let's go crazy, it is the holidays after all,' Ashley nods.

'We do have soda . . .' Dad offers, grabbing one for himself.

'Do you know how much sugar's in that?' Ashley says to my Dad.

'I'm not allowed soda any more,' Dylan says, looking enviously at the can. 'One day I drank fourteen in a row, I didn't sleep for seventy-two hours, and it turned my pee green,' she says, beginning to tremble.

'Hang on, she's got the sugar shakes again,' Ashley says. 'FLASH BACK ALERT! Give her something savoury to sniff, quick!'

I dive to the cupboard and grab the jar of olives. 'Clear!' I yell, before wafting one under her nose.

'Thank you,' Dylan mutters, as she begins to go back to normal.

'We thought we'd go into the den and take a look at the hologram phone I've been designing, maybe do some light algebra too,' I say to Dad.

'OK, but you can't be long, you've got to pack. Well you all have,' Dad says with a grin.

'Pack for what, Brian?' Ashley asks, flagrantly ignoring my 'no first name' policy.

'Camp—you're off to Happyville Summer Camp tomorrow, Tyler! And guess what? You girls are going with her!' he beams.

FRIENDS
UNTIL THE END
OF DAYS

'Summer Camp, are you kidding me, Brian? Sorry, I mean Brian, NO I MEAN DAD!' I yell. I think the idea of Summer Camp has short-circuited my brain.

'Oh come now Peach Weachy Pie . . . it's a few days, that's all.' Oh great, here come the fruit-based names, as if that's going to help.

'. . . it'll be fun, all those outdoor activities, it'll be wholesome. You'll be able to get in touch with

23

your inner you.'

'Inner you, what does that even mean?! Do you mean my innards, like my spleen? I don't want to touch my spleen!' I cry. 'And as for wholesome activities, you have met me right? I wanted to stay indoors all summer and play with my bacteria,' I say trying to appeal to his heart.

'Wait, wait . . .' Dylan interrupts. 'What did you mean when you said we were all going, Mr Tyler?' Dylan asks nervously. She gets embarrassed using grown-ups' names so she just calls Dad 'Mr' followed by my name.

'I've had a chat with all you kids' parents and they all think it's a good idea,' he grins, waving his phone about.

'DAMN YOU, PARENTS' WHATSAPP GROUP!'

Ashley says, shaking her fist towards the sky. 'I bet they've got wind that I was trying to sell them on eBay so that I could build an army of clones that only I control.'

'What?' Dad says.

'I said nice hair, Brian,' Ashley says, in a feeble attempt to cover her tracks.

'Oh thanks, it's the peppermint conditioner,' Dad says, totally buying it.

'This is an outrage. Why?! Why me! First we move to this weird town full of deadbeats . . .'

'No offence taken,' Dylan adds.

'You know what I mean,' I say. 'And now I have to go to Summer Camp. A place that is almost certainly worse than where I live. I'll have none of my stuff, I'll have to whittle things out of wood, eat what I find growing on trees, and pee in a hole.'

'Actually the facilities look charming,' he mumbles.

I ignore him and carry on. 'This is worse than awful. I'm sorry but this time you've gone too far. Dad, I'm afraid I'm not going and there's nothing you can do about it. Not one thing!'

((((⦿

'Pass me that suitcase,' I say to Ashley as we sit in the den packing.

'There you go,' she says, handing me the case. 'Who knew your dad had all the power—all he had to say was that he was going to cancel the broadband and you cracked,' Ashley helpfully points out. 'I mean, he really found your Achilles heel. You'd make a terrible soldier, you'd crack within the first five minutes. I don't think I'll be able to rely on you when the war comes.'

'War, what war?' I say, piling practically everything I own into my Scooby-Doo case.

'Ashley thinks that at some point humanity will implode and all law and order will break down,' Dylan adds, smiling sweetly.

'Only those who know how to use and control the robots will survive,' Ashley says, coldly.

'Ashley says I can be Emperor of the New Republic when we win, while she'll wield elegant power as Head of the Underground Police,' Dylan grins. 'Plus I'll get to wear a crown; it'll be so shiny and pretty!' Dylan squeals giddily.

'I'm afraid you'll be no good to me, Tyler. I can't have any weakness in my army of cyberwarriors,' she says, shaking her head.

'Well, can we be friends until the end of days? After that I promise not to hold you back.'

'Deal,' Ashley says, passing me my jacket to put in the suitcase. 'Wait, what's this?' she asks, pulling out a phone.

'Oh that's my phone! I call it the Hologramophone 2000—it's the one I've been inventing! It's lunar powered,' I say, showing off to the girls. 'It's basically an old smartphone but I used existing hologram technology so that it can project what's on screen. Imagine if you could open email attachments and look at them in 3D?!' I say, pressing a button. A strand of DNA pops up from the screen and I rotate it with my fingers to zoom in and out.

'Whoa!' Ashley and Dylan both coo.

'Apart from the name, it's amazing,' Ashley smiles.

'Did you say lunar powered?' Dylan asks.

'Yep, everything's solar powered these days, but no one ever thinks to use the moon. It's nearer, and it's just a question of using its gravitational and magnetic fields and turning them, via a simple transformer, into electricity. Plus, I'm the only one using the moon so I have it all to myself. It's like having a big battery floating in space. It's a bit temperamental mind— sometimes the phone can't deal with the moon's power. Last night, I was playing around with it when a text arrived and nearly burned off one of my eyebrows—plus I'm getting static electrical interference, so it needs a bit of work. That's why

I *was* looking forward to a summer in the den, fixing and fine-tuning,' I say sadly.

'Yeah, me too,' Ashley says.

'Yep, that would have been nice . . .' Dylan adds. 'Oh, I think I've found your bacterial experiment too—nice!' she says, picking up a cup.'

'Oh no, that's the milkshake I had last week, I wondered where that had gone.'

'Yuk, YUK, YU-U-U-U-K!' Dylan says throwing it down.

The next day I'm ready, I have my bag packed, seven types of coats, all the shoes I've ever owned, extra socks for warmth, and snow shoes—well you never know. Camping, even in the summer is rarely warm. I've even been working on my death stare to give to my dad as he drops me off.

'You're going to have great fun!' Dad says, trying to reassure me. 'I used to love Summer Camp when I was a kid. The great—'

'If you say "the great outdoors" one more time I'm going to puke. There is nothing great about the outdoors. It's cold, wet, and full of things with teeth and stings. The only reason I'm here is for my love—'

'Awww, well that means a lot to me,' Dad smiles.

'Please let me finish, the only reason I'm here is for my love of broadband,' I say, giving him my death stare.

He looks at me closely. 'Are you constipated, little peach?' he says. 'Ask if they have got some prune juice and do some jumping up and down. It always works for me.'

I can't even give him a good stare. Ashley's right, I'll be useless when the world ends.

A few minutes later, we pull up by a coach. Everyone from school is there. Basically what Dad's done is made me go to a portable version of school on the first day of my summer holiday. That's when it hits me. Courtney, oh my heck, she's going to be here too. Oh well this is just perfect. This is the worst thing that's ever happened to any human EVER!

Dad stops the car, and gets out. He's greeted by the other parents who are all giddy that they too are getting rid of their children for a week. They all smile and shake hands. How does my dad know so many people? Just how big is this WhatsApp group?! I think to myself. Then I feel a hand on my shoulder.

'I'm pretty sure this is how the war starts,' Ashley says. 'People using technology for their own foul purposes. It starts with a simple message about Summer Camp and before you know it, they are ruling the world. It might be time to awaken the sleeping army of rebels,' Ashley whispers in my ear. 'On the other hand I could be just reading too much into all this.'

'Ashley dear, don't forget your toothbrush.' I hear a voice, I turn round and it's Ashley's mum standing there. Ashley grabs it and puts in her knapsack. 'Do you have everything you need?' she says, trying to take a peek into Ashley's knapsack.

'I told you don't look in there, Bridgette,' Ashley says sternly.

'Mom, will you not call me mom, just once.'

'You'd like that wouldn't you, Bridgette. Well I don't play by the rules.' Ashley squints her eyes as if she's trying to work out if her mom is who she says she is.

'Oh, Ashley honey, we've been through this. I am your mother, you were not grown in a lab by a computer.'

'Hey guys!' I hear the familiar sound of Dylan's cheery voice. She's carrying two massive suitcases and a tiny bag on her back.

'Wow, how much did you pack? We're not going to need that many clothes,' I say, giving her a hand.

'Oh, no, my clothes are in my backpack, these are my medications and prescriptions. You can never be too careful,' she huffs. 'Hey, Mrs Ashley!' she says, waving at Ashley's mom.

'Where are your parents?' I ask.

'Oh well, you know, they were busy and it's only a half an hour walk from my house up a small hill, so I came on my own.'

'Well, what do you say, why don't we leave these kids to it, and we can grab a coffee?' my dad says to Ashley's mum in the single most icky moment I've ever seen in my life.

'Freedom coffee!' Ashley's mum laughs. 'Let's go into town. I need to get a new hairbrush— mine keep disappearing,' she says.

I look at Ashley. She mouths the words 'DNA testing' to me before adding, 'I think Subject One is on to me.'

As my dad and Ashley's mum head off, we take our seats on the bus.

'Rightio,' Dylan says, unpopping a lunch

box, 'I've had my travel sickness pills. Who wants a wrist band, eye mask, travel pillow, and a selection of sick bags?'

'I'll take an eye mask and a couple of the paper bags, please,' I reply.

'Rightio,' she says . . . dispensing them like a dealer handing out cards in a casino.

'This may be the most pathetic thing I've ever seen,' Courtney says, as her head pops up from the seat in front. 'I mean look at you, you can't even survive the coach journey without having to be medicated. You girls aren't going to last an hour, let alone a day.'

I should probably explain why Courtney hates me. She thinks I had a thing for her boyfriend Blane, or rather her ex-boyfriend— they have since separated because they want different things. She wants to be with someone who respects her while allowing her to grow as a person. Blane wants to not be going out with Courtney. That's why things didn't work out. Anyway, Courtney thinks that I liked Blane when they were together because I wanted to get close to him. I did want to get close to him, but only because his arm grew three feet during a football match and I needed to understand what had happened so I could stop all of mankind from suffering the same fate. Ever since then, Courtney has hated me.

'What a trio of scaredy cats.' Courtney shakes her head at us.

'Hey, maybe you should Change Me them.' Another head pops up—it's Tiffany, Courtney's best friend and an all-round jam head. 'Turn them into actual cats.'

'Change Me them?' I say. 'That doesn't even make sense.'

'Change Me!' Courtney says, looking horrified, like that's supposed to mean something. 'It's only the biggest thing ever.'

'The biggest thing ever? Bigger than the blue whale, a giant redwood, the Andromeda Galaxy . . .' I blurt.

'Big, like, you know, in the real world. Like on phones,' she says, pointing the camera at Ashley. 'Dweeboid is on the screen, I press this button and suddenly dweeboid has kitten ears.'

I peer at the screen. Sure enough there's Ashley with animal ears. 'Oh, you mean an algorithmic image-tracking application,' I sigh. Ashley starts tapping the top of her head, just to make sure she's earless.

'Yes, it's called Change Me! It's, like, more popular than cars or something, I think I read that on a tweet or something. I press this slider thing and her ears go from cute kitten to scary tiger.'

'There's a morphing button that allows the viewer to control the level of the graphic display,' I translate.

'Ohh . . .' Ashley and Dylan nod.

'Does it do unicorns!' Dylan says, trying to grab Courtney's phone.

'Hands off the merchandise,' Tiffany says.

'Err, yeah, totally, hands off the, like, merchandise,' Courtney says, holding it out of reach of Dylan. 'Only normal people are allowed to hold this.'

'Oh when will this beef end!' Dylan says sobbing wildly and thumping her fists against the back of the seat. 'Am I the only one who wants this war of words to finish? Can't we all be friends and learn to get on? Can't we get by without getting all up in each other's grill? Can't we!?'

'Oh god, I forgot how weird the little one

was. No. We are natural enemies, it's, like, the law of the jungle—you are sheep and I am the wolf. Don't you know anything? Tiffany, can I borrow your blusher? I feel I'm getting uglier by the second hanging around with these dorklings.' And with that the bus lurches off towards Summer Camp. I decide to put on my earphones, close my eyes, and let Beethoven soothe my nerves. Good old Beethoven.

)) ((◐

'Wake up, we're here!' Ashley says giving me a nudge. I open my eyes. There is the entrance. 'Welcome to Happyville Sumer Camp!' is carved into a wooden sign. There are carvings of wooden animals everywhere I look, cute squirrels, chipmunks, and rabbits, all grinning like they're

44

on some sort of medication. All around there are kids in hats and shorts, some with maps out, some gathering firewood, and worst of all, some are communal singing. I can see obstacle courses amongst the trees, I can make out a lake too, with some kids rowing in boats, while others jump into the water or play sports. It's literally like someone took my worst nightmare and made it real. I scan around but I can't see a library anywhere. Where are the science labs—do summer camps have science labs? But all those questions fade away when I see who's standing there waiting for us. 'No, NO IT CAN'T BE!'

BEWARE
OF PEOPLE WITH RHYMING NAMES

'Tyler, is that you?' a couple say to me through the window as the bus jolts to a halt.

'No, it can't be!' I scream in my head. But it is . . . 'Hi Pipper, hi Kipper,' I say as best I can, my grin as fixed as theirs.

OK, it's time for a recap. Well, you remember that before I came to Happyville I used to live in the big city? Well I didn't really go to school there, because of my big

brain. Now, I know how that sounds like I'm a
big show-off who thinks she's cleverer than
everyone else. Well, I promise I'm not a show-
off. I am, however, cleverer than everyone else.
This is just a fact. Now, if it helps, having an IQ
that's off the scale isn't that much fun. People
tend to either call you a freak or want you to
help them with their homework, it's just the
way it goes. Anyway, being the blurter that I
am, I have either told every teacher that I ever
met that I know more than them, or stayed
at home because I can learn more that way.
So Dad decided that maybe a home tutor
was the way to go, and we tried out a few
different candidates. It was a disaster. There
was Mr Carothers who fell asleep halfway

through day one, so he had to go. There was Miss Kurov, who turned out to be on the run from the police for armed robbery, so she didn't last long either. Then there was Kipper and Pipper—all I'll say is beware of married couples with rhyming names. They had a new approach to teaching—it was basically a lot of singing with a guitar, doing 'hand hugs' where you link fingers with each other and smile lots. They also believed that the best way to improve was to get in touch with your spirit animal. There was a lot of yoga, meditation, herbal tea, and huge amounts of quinoa. It was, as you can imagine, awful. I vowed then and there that I would do things my own way from then on. If I wanted to read a book, I

would, despite what my 'inner squirrel' needed.
So Pipper and Kipper went and Dad stepped
in. And now they're back in my life, with the
same beige and pastel wardrobe.

'Who are those two?' Dylan asks.

'New Age types. I've met them before,'
I say. 'They're all about hugging and singing
about flowers,' I say.

'Oh my,' Ashley shudders as we begin to
pile out of the bus. 'If you take me home now
. . . achhhhooooo!' she sneeze-yells to the
driver who's busy unloading the bags, 'I will
give you my shoes!' she says in desperation.
'Achooo! The animal allergies have started,' she
whimpers.

'Huh?' he says looking confused.

'OK, you can be commander of the robots in my new government,' Ashley says, begging him.

'I just drive the bus, lady,' he says, edging away.

'Well, looky who we have here, Pipper.'

'I know Kipper!' Oh my, I had forgotten how they say each other's names all the time. It sets my nerves jangling.

'It's Tyler Fitz, the girl who thinks she's really smart and too good to get in touch with her inner spirit animal,' they say smiling.

'No, no it's not that, I just like reading books,' I reply.

'You can't get everything from a book,' Kipper says.

'You can when it's maths,' I say, making what I think is a very good point. 'It's one of those subjects that require little or no singing.'

'Oh, are you still going on about maths?' Courtney joins in. This is great, all I need is my mad dead Aunt Mary and Stalin to turn up and it'll be all the people I hate most in the world in one place.

'For the last time, they've discovered all the numbers, humans have completed maths,' Courtney says, as she heads to greet Kipper and Pipper.

'Hello, Big Squirrel Pipper and Big Squirrel Kipper,' she says, before performing some sort of strange handshake-cum-salute.

'Hello, Raccoon Courtney!' they both beam.

'What was that?' Ashley says. 'They're grown-ups, why are they talking like toddlers?!' Ashley whimpers, before turning to the driver again. 'I'll throw in my own kidney and several members of my family if you take me with you.' Which only scares the driver away even quicker.

'I see you've managed to get some friends,' Pipper says, looking at Dylan and Ashley.

'Your t-shirt's the colour of mucus!' Dylan says, shaking their hands.

'Oh my . . . !' Pipper says.

'I am Ashley,' Ashley says, looking Pipper and Kipper up and down. 'You stay out of my way and you won't get hurt. Now what's the WiFi code? In fact, it doesn't matter, I'll just hack in myself.'

'I can see why you three are friends,' Pipper says, trying not to look horrified. 'There is no WiFi code, there are no computers, all guests are asked to hand in their phones on arrival,' Pipper says, holding out a box for us to put our handsets in. 'We are about being outdoor campers this week, but we may allow some phone time for those who are good. I know it's hard keeping on top of one's social diary,' she says, giving Courtney a knowing wink. 'Don't think of yourselves as humans . . .'

'I know I certainly don't,' Courtney sneers.

'. . . we are all just woodland creatures, here to have fun and express our inner feelings.'

'I'm having some pretty strong inner feelings right now,' Ashley says. 'Give me a rolling pin and I'll express them on your head.'

'You are wasting your breath, Big Squirrels,'

Courtney says. 'These three aren't like normal people. They are hopeless. Am I in Raccoon Lodge as normal? I hope the hot tub is warm, I'm feeling very tense after the journey.'

'Yes you are dear, we'll see you at the introduction in half an hour, it'll give you chance to unpack. Where's the rest of your stuff?'

'One of my fellow raccoons will be bringing it,' Courtney says clapping her hands at Tiffany.

'What cabin are we in?' I ask.

'Woodlouse,' Pipper answers. 'Meet us by the campfire in 30 minutes.'

As the bus pulls away I finally take in the whole camp. As I stroll through the ornate wooden gates and into the forest I see cabins all around. There are a few strange looks from

the other campers as I wheel my case in.
Like I'm an interloper trying to sneak into a
private party. In the middle is a clearing where
a campfire is being prepared. One cabin says
'canteen' on the door, the others seem to
have animal names written on. The sun shines
through the tall trees: it looks perfect, in a
painting sort of way. Yes, this would make a
lovely painting. Through the trees I see the
blue shimmering lake, I can hear the distant
splashing of paddles hitting the water. There
are climbing ropes and zip wires hanging
between the trunks. My case's wheels get
stuck in the dirt as I try and pull it along, and
as I look and see the dirt being ploughed
I make a mental note of the many creepy

crawlies that I can see wandering around.
It's as if the ground is alive. The cabins are
all perfectly crafted and full of excited kids
unpacking, giggling, and reuniting with old
friends. There is only one cabin left—it sits in
a pile of moss in the shadows. I look at Ashley
and Dylan, and sure enough, my fears are
correct. It's ours all right.

As the door opens it creaks like we're
about to enter a haunted house. The dorm is
like a prison camp, bare walls, and cold metal
bunks greet us. I look around and smile sadly.
'At least we're among our own,' I mutter. Here
are all the other misfits: it's the cabin out of
the way, the one that's hidden in the shadows.
The one where they put the coughers and the

weepers, the place where the kids with thick specs stay, children with constant runny noses and notes from their mum. The ones who have to wear thermal vests all year round, the ones who get glue ear at the first sign of drizzle. We find some bunks and start to unpack.

'This place is definitely, absolutely, worse than my house,' I huff. 'There isn't even a basic library.'

'You can't read here,' one girl says. She has glasses on, one lens covered over with a patch. 'They'll take your books away from you. Someone brought a copy of *Lord of the Flies* a couple of years back and there was a mini uprising, so they cracked down pretty hard. But if it's reading material you're after, I may be able to get you something,' she says, tapping her nose. 'I'm friendly with one of the chefs—they might be able to loan you a tin of soup. The ingredients list is pretty extensive.'

'Food? Food is the only thing in this place you can read?'

'Yep. Welcome to Summer Camp. Oh, I'm Peggy by the way.'

'I'm Fitz, this is Dylan and Ashley,' I say pointing at the other two.

'I'm averagely pleased to make your acquaintance. Please don't take my pleasantness for friendship. I have as many friends as I'll ever need, you'll be wasting your time if you grew to like me,' Ashley says, holding out her hand.

'I like your glasses, you look like a pirate!' Dylan giggles.

'I can see why they put you three with us.' Peggy says.

'Is there anything you are allowed here?' I ask.

'Some people are allowed phones, but only

if they earn enough Happy

Points,' Peggy says.

'What's a "Happy

Point"?' I ask nervously.

'YOU GET THEM FOR

PLAYING BY THE RULES,' a boy

suddenly yells. 'SUCKING UP TO THE

MAN, BEING HAPPY CAMPERS. EXCELLING AT

THEIR LITTLE GAMES. I'M HERBERT!' he shouts.

'Wow, OK,' I say.

'I HAVE AN EAR INFECTION SO

EVERYTHING'S A BIT MUFFLED, SO

SOMETIMES I SHOUT. I THOUGHT I SHOULD

WARN YOU!' Herbert yells.

'YOU'RE DOING IT NOW!' Peggy yells back

at him.

'DO YOU WANT TO BE MY GIRLFRIEND!' he shouts over at Ashley. 'I CAN TELL YOU AND I ARE THE SAME, MAVERICKS IN THIS TWO-BIT TOWN!' he screams.

'What's he doing, why is he looking at me like that?' Ashley asks.

'I think someone has a little crush,' Peggy says, shaking her head at Herbert.

'A crush, what you mean like . . . Oh my, that's disgusting.' Ashley screws up her face at the very horror of it. 'I DON'T LIKE YOU. I DON'T REALLY LIKE PEOPLE. YOU REPULSE ME!' Ashley shrieks back at him.

'TELL ME, DO YOU LIKE ROCKS?' he winks. 'I KNOW WHERE WE CAN GO AND LOOK AT ROCKS!' Herbert bellows.

'Oh no,' she sighs. 'This is going to be a long few days.'

'Whoa!' Dylan says, spotting my hologram phone in my bag. 'You brought it with you!' she claps with excitement.

'Well I thought I could do some work on it. You know, in secret. It might stop me going mad. Don't tell, I don't want to hand it over.'

'CRIKEY THIS IS AN AMAZING PHONE, I HAVEN'T SEEN ONE LIKE THIS EVER. YOU BEST KEEP IT A SECRET!' he screams.

'WELL STOP SHOUTING ABOUT IT THEN!' Dylan yells back.

'I've never seen a phone like this before. Where did you get it?' Peggy asks.

'I made it, I call it the Hologramophone

2000 . . . well, I *think* I do, I'm still undecided.'

'That's so cool. What apps do you have for it?' Peggy asks.

'Apps. I don't do apps. Plus it's a bit shaky, it's only a prototype.'

'Do the ears app. Ears!!' Dylan squeals. 'Please, I love ears!'

'No! You have ears already. Just use a mirror.'

'It's not the same,' Dylan sighs. 'What's this place like anyway?' she asks Peggy and Herbert.

'Awful, I mean it's really weird, the people who run it are weird and the other kids hate us,' Peggy sighs. 'I'm in charge of the escape committee, do you want in? We Woodlice try to stick together, that way it's harder for them to pick us off. I got the idea from a documentary I watched about sharks.'

'Are we the sharks? Please tell me that we're the sharks in this analogy!' I cry.

'I LIKE TO STAY IN THE CABIN AS MUCH AS POSSIBLE. THEY SAY THESE WOODS ARE HAUNTED, THEY SAY THAT IT'S NOT SAFE OUT THERE AFTER DARK, THEY SAY . . .'

'Can I just ask, who's "they"?' Ashley says, interrupting.

'ERRR . . . SOME OF THE KIDS.' Herbert stutters.

'Do you mean you?' Ashley says, pressing him.

'NO, WELL, YES I SUPPOSE. BUT I'M SERIOUS, THERE'S SOMETHING AWFUL STALKING THESE PARTS . . .'

'We know, it's Pipper and Kipper,' I add.

'NO, SOMETHING HAIRY WITH MAD EYES AND A VILE ODOUR.'

'Yes, I think that's still Pipper and Kipper and their aromatherapy kit,' I say.

'NOOOOO!' Herbert snaps. 'THESE HILLS ARE SPOOKY, IT TURNS NORMAL PEOPLE INTO DANGEROUS CREATURES. I'VE SEEN WHAT THESE WOODS CAN DO TO PEOPLE . . .'

'Herbert has been a regular all his life,' Peggy says. 'He likes to think of himself as the camp expert around here. He has quite an imagination.'

'I THOUGHT I HEARD HOWLS OF PAIN IN THE NIGHT!' Herbert says, looking off into the distance.

'I think a squirrel has misplaced his nuts,'

Peggy whispers.

'I think that'd make me howl too,' Dylan adds.

'JUST BEWARE, THAT'S ALL . . .' Herbert

adds, ominously.

WHOOOOOOOOOW HOOOOOOOOOOOO!

A siren screams, causing us all to jump out of

our skins.

'INDUCTION TIME!' Herbert cries, clapping

his hands.

THE STORM LEG STRIKES BACK

'Welcome to Happyville Summer Camp, a spiritual and healing retreat for young people,' Kipper tells us at the induction a few minutes later. 'The camp has been divided into different cabins. Foxes who are wily and brave.' There's a huge cheer from one section of kids, presumably the foxes amongst us. 'Raccoons who are smart and tenacious.'

'Hurray!'

'Eagles who soar high!'

'Hurrah!'

'And Woodlice are also here.' We murmur and mumble sarcastic cheers. 'The aim for us is to have fun, discover our inner woodland creature, become at one with nature, make new friends, and learn to love nature. Some of the fun activities we'll be doing here include, sailing, tree climbing, flower pressing, singing, jam making, whittling art sculptures, water volleyball. As well as exploring feeling in the emotionary tent, art therapy in the rainbow wigwam, and poncho weaving in the craft cabin. Any questions? Yes, you at the back.'

'Does anyone have a big pair of pliers?' Ashley asks aloud. 'I'd like to pull my own head off.'

'I see we have a lively Woodlouse, let's hope you don't get trampled, dear,' Pipper says sternly. 'And remember the more Happy Points you get for your cabin, the more treats you get!'

'And now for the camp anthem,' Kipper says, pulling out a guitar and strumming a

chord. 'I'mmmm aaaa happy, furry, hoppy, jumpy, cutesy, waggy, leapy, nibbly, little beastie . . . !'

I've never heard so many adjectives put to music. Eight and a half horrid hours later we have finished our first day at the camp. I have climbed, canoed, whittled, sung, learnt an utterly pointless and over-complicated handshake, eaten a picnic up a tree, and lost several 'Happy Points' for my cabin (apparently trying to flag down a passing motorist to tell them we've been kidnapped by the fun police doesn't go down too well here). Every bone in my body aches, including all the ones in my ears. My body is not used to putting up with this amount of physical pain. I lost Dylan and

Ashley at the second circuit of the assault course. All I want is my bed, preferably one in a hospital, but I will take a rusty one in my cabin all the same. I climb on my bunk and scratch a dash into the wall. 'Day One: done,' I sigh. Just at that second, Ashley troops through the door, mud on her face, eyes filled with pain.

'What's wrong with the world? I thought this was supposed to be Summer Camp. Did I miss something, did we tick the wrong box and somehow we've joined the marines? EVERYTHING ACHES! Including my ears . . .' she sighs.

'Yes! Me too. How did that happen?!' I say, rubbing them.

'I think it's all that singing,' Ashley shrugs.

'I'm going to go for a lie down and wait for the sweet relief of death to come,' she says. 'Do you have anything to eat? I want my last meal to be something more than berries.'

'I've got a few bread rolls and biscuits that I grabbed during lunch. Let me get them for you.'

'You're a good friend. Where's Dylan?' she asks.

'I don't know,' I answer, grabbing my bag from under my bunk. 'I saw her running away when the tambourines came out. The other Woodlice are just finishing up the last of the singing then they'll be over.'

Just at that second there's a howl of wind from outside. I look out. 'Looks like we made it just in time,' I say, looking out of the window to see that the trees are swaying in the wind, and a dark cloud is creeping across the sky, almost covering the bright moon. 'It looks like there's a storm coming in.' Just at that moment Ashley's right leg starts tap-dancing by itself. That's right, tap-dancing, but only the one leg—it's possibly the strangest thing I've ever seen. 'Are you all right?'

'Oh, it's a bad storm too,' Ashley says, confidentially.

'What the hell's the matter with you, and

how do you know?!' I ask, aghast, as she starts
to hop around the cabin like she's trying to
stamp out an imaginary fire.

'My leg always starts doing this whenever
there's a storm on its way. I call it my storm
leg. You know how cows lie down in a field
when it's going to rain? Well, this is the same,
except without cows and located in my leg.'

'I've got to take a picture of this!' I say.
Where's my hologram phone? This will look
amazing in 3D,' I say, riffling around in my case.

'Please, no publicity!' Ashley begs. 'This is

going to do my application to Harvard no good at all.'

'Oh my, someone's been in here.' There's no phone. 'Someone's stolen it! We've been robbed!' I yell.

'Wait, can you hear something?' Ashley hushes me, jumping to her feet, or her feet jumping to her, I'm not quite sure. 'I can hear something.'

At first I hear nothing, then I hear a strange chuckling and clicking sound.

'I think it's coming from inside the bathroom.' Ashley points. We both creep over and listen.

'I think there's someone in there!' I whisper.

'Do you think it's the robber?' Ashley asks,

still tap-dancing away, but in a really quiet tip-toey sort of way—it's quite impressive.

'Well I do now!'

'Or an axe murderer!' Ashley whispers.

'Stop saying words,' I yell.

'OK, after three,' Ashley says, 'One . . . two . . . three!'

'What? What are we supposed to do after three?' I ask. 'That really wasn't specific.'

'Oh, I meant storm the bathroom.'

'Oh, all right.'

'One . . . two—'

'Hey guys!' Dylan says, coming out of the door. 'What are you two doing sneaking around?'

'AGGGH!' Ashley and I cry. 'I thought

you were . . . oh never mind. Hey, is that my phone?' I ask, looking at Dylan's hand.

'Yeah, I hope you don't mind, I was looking for a snack in your bag—I hope you don't mind that either—when I spotted your phone. I wanted to get a closer look at it, I was interested in the way you've plotted the user interface.'

'But we heard laughing,' Ashley says.

I take the phone off Dylan and look at the screen. 'Change Me!' I say, 'Oh Dylan, I thought you were better than this, you've been looking for unicorn filters on that app Courtney was using!'

'I'm sorry, I just really, really like unicorns! Look!' she says, holding the phone in front of

herself and firing up the
app. Suddenly, holographic
unicorn ears and a sparkly
horn appear on Dylan's
head, and when she moves,
the ears and horn move too.

I have to admit, it looks pretty cool. 'You could

make a fortune, Fitz,' Dylan says. 'Look, they

have other animals too, cats . . .' she presses

the button on the screen and cute cat ears and

whiskers appear, 'squirrels,' she transforms

again, sprouting two large front teeth and

fluffy red ears, 'and they have scary creatures

too, like a dinosaur, or a dog . . . But I think

there's something wrong with the way it's

using the lunar power. You basically designed

the transformer too well. It can't cope with the supply. It's like using a power station to run a toaster off. Look,' she says grabbing the phone again.

'Well, it's only a prototype, please be careful, it's not stable yet.'

'Yeah, sure,' Dylan says, ignoring me and getting more and more excited. 'If you alter the digital signal processor by 10% you should be able to adjust the power control setting.'

Just at that second Ashley's leg begins to swing round and her hair goes spiked. 'Oh my, the storm is very near!' There's a clap of thunder and a flash of lightning. Rain begins to beat down on the windows. 'It's basically on top of us!'

'Yeah, anyway, like I was saying, the analogue and digital conversion rates are easy to change.'

'Dylan!' I yell. 'There's too much static, turn it off, you might overload it! It's not used to using third party apps,' I cry. I can see the phone beginning to light up and bleep. The two aerials on the top begin to shake.

'What?!' she yells, as the noise of the rain on the windows begins to drown me out. Louder and louder it gets as Ashley's leg hits the ground over and over again. I feel like we're in the eye of the storm, you can feel it on your teeth, the taste of electricity as the air becomes charged, and just when the tension becomes almost too unbearable,

CRACK!

For a few seconds all I can hear is a high-pitched whistle. It's dark. I can smell slightly singed wood. We must have been hit by lightning. Then from nowhere there's a sound, a terrible sound.

'HOOOOOWWWWWWWWWWWLLLLL!'

'DYLAN ARE YOU ALL RIGHT!' I shriek, trying to get my bearings. I hold my hands out—I can feel something. . .

'Ow!'

I recognize the voice. It's Ashley.

'Are you OK?' I yell.

'No, you've just poked me in the nose,' she snaps.

'Sorry! Dylan, where are you, what was that noise, are you hurt?'

I grab the phone and pick it up. It's still glowing so I use what light it's giving off as a torch. Through the screen Ashley and I can see Dylan get to her feet and look at us. 'Are you OK?' I ask.

Dylan blinks, and rubs her head. On the phone screen is a startled picture of Dylan with puppy ears. Just at that second the lights come back on. 'Someone must have fixed the fuse,' I say. The phone blinks on and off again once, before finally bleeping and dying in my hands.

'Can it be repaired?' Ashley asks.

'I don't know, it looks like the static from the storm blew some of the components out. I can smell them, they're burnt out.'

'Oh I'm sorry,' Dylan says, 'I just wanted a play.'

'It's OK. I'm sure we can fix it once we're homaaaaaaaaRRRGH!' I shriek.

'Once we're what?' Ashley says, looking

at me. I dart my eyes towards Dylan, willing Ashley to look over and see what I've just seen.

'When we're homeaaaargh,' Dylan repeats helpfully. 'I think she means home: it's pronounced home. H. O. M. E.'

Ashley looks over at her, her eyes widen for a split second and then she looks back at me. We both look at Dylan once again. There she is, standing in front of us, with dog ears attached to the top of her head. Not on a phone or a computer screen, but in real life. Our best friend is a walking, talking, human puppy.

THE GREAT SHED DISASTER

For a second Ashley and I say nothing, we just stare open-mouthed at Dylan. She seems fine, I mean she isn't obviously in pain, apart from that blood-curdling howl, obviously. They aren't bothering her. I mean she has no idea that they're there, but she just seems fine, normal, good old happy Dylan. It's like being worried about a piano falling from the top of a skyscraper and landing on your head. Yes, if you knew it was falling, you'd be quite bothered. But if you were walking along happily minding your own business and didn't know that a piano was about to fall on your head, you wouldn't be bothered about it at all. Right up until the moment that you were turned into a pink smear on the pavement. This is a falling piano and Ashley and I have to find a way of dealing with it without Dylan looking up. But, in the meantime, I should probably say something to Dylan, because all the time I've been thinking about pianos I've just been staring at her with my mouth open. Dylan gets up and dusts herself off.

'What do we do?' I whisper over to Ashley. 'Shall we tell her?'

'NO!' Ashley snaps back. 'Dylan is a panicker. Once, she had to be lassoed after she went on the rampage when a bee landed on her jumper. She took out several flowerbeds and a shed.'

'So, what—we don't tell her?' I ask. 'I'm thinking she's going to find out eventually!'

'Look, we don't know how long this will last—maybe the ears will fade away in a minute? Let's not tell her till we know for sure,' Ashley says.

'What are you two whispering about?' Dylan asks.

'Ohmyohmyohmy!' I repeat. 'Oh my. OH MY! Oh my . . . it is cold, what with that storm blowing in ear. I mean, 'ear'. I mean in heeeere!

With an 'h'. Isn't it cold, Ashley?' I say, shooting her a look as if to say please agree with me.

'Yes. Yes. I mean yes,' Ashley nods. 'The weather. Yes, the weather,' Ashley says trying to form words.

'We should probably wrap up warm, all that rain and wind you know, put a hat on . . .' I say, winking at Ashley.

'HATS!' Ashley suddenly yells, getting it finally. 'Put on a hat, Dylan put on a hat! Please tell me you have a hat? I will knit you one if you don't have one!'

'I have a hat, obviously,' Dylan says slowly looking at Ash and me as if we're very odd indeed. 'I don't go camping without a hat, in fact I don't go anywhere without a hat. But are you sure, the storm seems to have passed now.'

At that second Ashley begins to wave her leg around wildly. 'Nope, I think there's a bit more storm out there,' she says, pointing at her foot. 'You need a hat, we all need hats!'

'Gosh, okay, I'll go pick out a bobble,' Dylan says wandering over to her bunk.

'Great, us too! Let's all go and put hats on and keep them on for a really long time. Crikey, I love a hat!' I yell, as Dylan walks off towards her bunk.

'OMG she has dog ears!' I whisper-scream. 'And she has no idea!'

'I know. We don't know what those things are, or what they might do. They might spread, you might be able to catch them! I don't want to catch ears, no thank you!' Ashley says shaking her head. 'It's standard scientific procedure to quarantine and examine, so that's what we should do.'

'I thought you said they might go in a few minutes!'

'Well they might, Fitz, but I don't know, they may last a lifetime. This isn't something I've dealt with before!' Ashley snaps. 'We need to—'

'Yes I know, quarantine and examine,

although I'm not sure a bobble hat is the best way to isolate a potentially dangerous outbreak,' I huff.

'You haven't seen her when she freaks out, it's like a bucking bronco with pigtails.'

'To be fair, I think even the most mild-mannered person would freak out if they got hit by lightning and grew animal ears.'

'You make an excellent point!' Ashley agrees.

'But we can't not tell her,' I say, 'because, and there's really no way around this, she's going to find out. Having dog ears on the top of your head is the sort of thing one tends to notice,' I whisper-scream at Ashley.

'Another good point,' she adds. 'We are

making excellent points here today. Considering the situation, the fact that we are managing to be so rational is a very good sign.'

'Too true. I mean I want to run into the forest and scream for about ten minutes straight, but the good news is that I haven't done that yet, so I also feel that's a good sign.'

'We need to get a closer look,' Ashley whispers.

'I mean, it might be something that you can pull off? You know like plucking a ripe peach from a tree.'

'Maybe you're right, perhaps we could take them off and flush them down the toilet for instance?' I suggest.

'Exactly!' Ashley agrees.

'Great. Go for it,' I say patting her on the shoulder.

'Why me?' Ashley protests. 'I don't want to touch her freaky animal ears. What if my hand turns into a deformed claw or something? Plus, it's your phone, you're the one that turned her into a human dog person, you're like a witch!' Ashley whisper-shrieks at me. 'The others will be back any moment. They're going to notice and say something,' Ashley says, peeking out of the window.

'Fine. You distract her, I'll try and pull her dog ears off and flush them down the toilet . . . I bet that's a sentence that no one else has ever said in the history of the world.'

'How's the hat thing coming along Dylan?'

Ashley asks, pulling on one that she happened to have in her rucksack.

'I have one, it's multi-coloured, it's like dipping your head in a rainbow!' Dylan yells excitedly, waving her rainbow hat around in her hand.

'Ooh, can I see, I have hat envy!' Ashley says cheerfully.

While Ashley and Dylan compare hats, I stand behind Dylan and tentatively I reach out with the tips of my fingers and pull at Dylan's new ears, being as gentle as I can be just in case it hurts. But it's no good, my fingers go right through—it's like putting my hands through a ghost, like they are made of electricity. There's nothing to grab! Ashley looks at me and shrugs, as if to say 'now what?'

'Let's tell her . . .' I mouth back. I open my
mouth so I can say something when just at that
second we hear voices from outside. It sounds
as though the others are coming back.

'YES!' Dylan yells and bolts to the window,
pressing her nose against the glass. 'THE
OTHERS ARE COMING. I LOVE THOSE GUYS,
I'M JUST SOOOOOO EXCITED!'

'What are we going to do?' I say to Ashley.

'We need to get that hat on fast! Operation Bobble Hat Quarantine is on,' I say, turning to Dylan.

'OK, everyone got their hats on? We don't want anyone getting a cold now do we?'

'Aw, Fitz, you're so kind to look out for me like this,' Dylan smiles, popping on her prize bobble.

'No problemo!' I grin. 'Great, then I guess that means we can let them in.'

'I'd forgotten how much I love hats!' Dylan says jumping up and down. 'Look they're almost here!'

'Hey guys,' Peggy says opening the door.

'PEGGY! I LOVE PEGGY!!' Dylan barks.

Yes you heard me, she barked it out.

'HELLO DYLAN,' Herbert yells back.

'HERBERT. HE'S HERE TOO!' Dylan jumps
up and licks his face.

'Why are you shouting?' Peggy asks Dylan.
'Do you have an ear infection too.'

'WHY IS SHE LICKING ME, WHY IS DYLAN
LICKING ME?' Herbert asks, looking grossed
out.

'She's hungry, it's the great outdoors, it makes everyone peckish. That's all,' I say.

'WELL EATING FELLOW CAMPERS IS AGAINST THE RULES. IT SAYS SO IN PARAGRAPH 4B. I DON'T LIKE THE REGIME HERE EITHER, BUT I HAVE TO SAY I AGREE WITH THAT ONE.'

'I *am* hungry!' Dylan says, 'Gosh I could murder some sausages. Does anyone have any? What about a steak?' she says sniffing around.

'You know what, I think we've all had a big day, a lot of excitement. I think the storm has made us all a little freaky. Why don't we all go to bed, turn off the lights and no one say anything until dawn,' I suggest to my fellow Woodlouse campers, trying desperately to distract them from Dylan's behaviour.

'YES!' Ashley agrees in a very obvious way.

There are a few mumbles of discontent and
then people start to nod too.

'NO DYLAN, FOR THE LOVE OF MIKE,
NOOOOOO!!!!' I scream, before diving across the
floor to get to the toilet door just in time to stop
Dylan opening it.

'What?' she asks, looking utterly bewildered.

'Let's not bother with all that, let's just go
to sleep,' I say, trying to keep her away from the
mirror by the sink. I can't risk her discovering
her transformation before bed. 'Just bed, no
teeth brushing, it'll be like we're animals.'

'Er, OK, but I think the storm sent you a little
freaky too,' Dylan whispers under her breath as

she turns and heads towards her bunk.

'How on earth are we going to keep this up?' Ashley asks, helping me to my feet. 'We're here for two more days! And is it just me or is—'

'No it's not you, she's behaving like a puppy,' I confirm. 'Look, I'm sure it'll go soon, it's just a temporary animal behavioural syndrome,' I say, grabbing the phone and trying to turn it on. 'No, it's no good, the thing is burnt out. Do you think we can repair it?' I ask Ashley.

'I mean, I've got a few things in my rucksack, but it's not going to be easy.'

NERDLINGS
IN DESCENDING
ORDER

'Hoooooooooooowl!'

I wake from my sleep. I must have been
dreaming about Dylan—I'm even hearing howls
in my sleep. I rub the sleep from my eyes and
blink until my eyes are used to the sunshine.
Last night's storm has gone and I can hear
the birds singing. It looks like it's going to be
a beautiful day. It's amazing how suddenly
everything feels different in daylight: problems

that were huge the previous night are suddenly smaller, manageable. There's nothing a dose of sunshine can't fix.

'Fitz, wake up!' Ashley says looming over me.

'Yikes, what is it?' I say. I'm not used to Ashley's face being so close to mine at this time of the day.

'It's Dylan, she's gone,' Ashley tells me. OK, so there are some things that a dose of sunshine can't fix.

'What? Are you kidding me?'

'That's not all,' Ashley says. 'I think I just heard a howl coming from the woods.'

'Oh no, I thought that was a dream.' I get out of bed and follow Ashley to where Dylan's bunk is. It's still early and no one's really awake yet. I look over at Dylan's bed: there's nothing there. The blanket and pillow are all gone. Then Ashley points to the corner of the cabin by the radiator—there's a blanket and pillow. Dylan's blanket and pillow.

'So much for hoping that she's all better,' Ashley says, raising an eyebrow.

'It might be a coincidence?' I say helpfully.

'She's got up in the night to sleep in the corner by the radiator!' Ashley says pointedly. 'Does this sound like the sort of thing, say, a person would do? Does it sound like the sort of thing a chicken would do?' Ashley asks.

'A chicken, no of course not.'

'That's because she's not a chicken, she's a puppy!' Ashley says.

She's right, the hope that Dylan would wake up and everything would be all right again was a silly notion. 'What do you think happened?'

'I don't know,' Ashley says. 'Maybe she woke up, saw that she had ears and ran away, you know, into the woods because of the shame of it all, never to be seen again. I mean, I would,' Ashley adds unhelpfully.

'Come on, my Uncle had a puppy. Puppies are easy to handle, they just need play and attention. I'm sure we can do that—between the two of us we can handle a puppy,' I say, grabbing a handful of biscuits. 'We need to go and find her before anyone else does,' I say. 'Let's get dressed.'

◖◖ ◖◉

A few minutes later we are outside in the bright sunshine. The camp is beginning to stir. I can see girls and boys beginning to emerge into the sunshine, off with toothbrushes and towels to shower blocks, getting ready for the day's action.

'Well look what animal I've found!' I freeze, turn round, and see Pipper smiling at me. 'It's a wandering Woodlouse. Where are you off to at this hour? I would have thought you'd want to stay inside. I know how you love to be inside out of harm's way.'

'Good morning Big Squirrel Pipper,' I say with a grin, despite the fact I've

> a) just greeted another human being as a squirrel and

> b) that human is a grown-up.

Why is it that the older people get, the more like kids they are.

'Ashley and I were just off to collect some delicious leaves for breakfast for our fellow Woodlice. We'll need a hearty feed for another big day of squishy, happy, furry, bouncy fun!' I say, waving my hand in the time-honoured secret camp handshake-salute-thingy, trying to get rid of Pipper as quickly as possible.

'About time too. I knew there was a Woodlouse in you, Tyler.'

'Ew,' Ashley says, wrinkling her nose.

'You should take a leaf out of your friend's book.'

'Our friend's book—who do you mean?' I say, looking at Ashley.

'You know, the other one?' Pipper says.

'Other one?' Ashley asks.

'Yes, oh do I have to spell it out? The other member of the geeky trinity,' she says, rolling her eyes. 'There's the tall, skinny nerd, the middle one, and the little nerdling. You three come as quite a package of oddballs. You are the tall skinny one, Fitz is the middle-sized one, and the *other* one is the little one, that's the one I'm talking about. You should take a leaf out of her book, she's been up for hours!'

'You know, come the end of days, I'll make sure they come for you first,' Ashley whispers in Pipper's ear.

'Have a good day, Big Squirrel!' I grin, and pull Ashley away.

'I don't like bullies,' Ashley snarls, especially squirrelly ones.

'Nor me, let's deal with her later. First we need to find Dylan before—'

'WHAAAAACHOOOOOOOO!' Ashley sneezes.

'Before what?' Dylan asks.

Ashley and I turn round. 'You're OK, you're alive!' I say, delightedly.

'Why would I not be alive?' Dylan asks.

'How do you feel?' Ashley asks, looking

her up and down. 'I see you've still got the hat on?'

'Oh have I?' Dylan laughs, 'I forgot about that. I feel fine. I mean the storm was a bit weird, I think we were all a little, you know, silly last night. I know you two were, maybe I was too. It had just been a long day. I feel fine. Never better in fact!'

'Oh,' I say, looking at Ashley. 'Maybe all that stuff from last night has disappeared today,' I whisper to Ashley.

'Yes, maybe everyone is back to normal today. Can I just see under your hat, Dylan?' Ashley asks casually.

'Oh you two and your hat obsession. Enough of the hat chat already!' Dylan chuckles. Ashley and I chuckle too, robotically, trying to work out if there is a pair of ears under there.

'So, where have you been?' I ask changing the subject.

'Oh, it was such a beautiful day I thought I'd go for a run. So what time's breakfast?' Dylan smiles.

'I'm sorry I thought you said *run*,' Ashley says, leaning in to hear properly.

'Yes I said run,' Dylan smiles.

'Sorry, can you say that again. I heard *run*, did anyone else hear *run* again?' Ashley says.

'I did say run!' Dylan giggles.

'But you never run,' I say to Dylan. 'It makes you feel sick, like sport and people who believe in astrology!'

'Well, today I just felt like it. Plus I brought you back a present too,' Dylan says reaching into her pockets. 'Now hold out your hands!' she says, grinning.

Ashley and I both hold out our hands and look at Dylan.

'There you go!' Dylan says, beaming.

'A stick! You've fetched us a stick!' I cry. 'Look, Ashley, Dylan is fetching us sticks. She's retrieving sticks!'

'Not just any stick. Look at it, have you ever seen a more beautiful stick in your life, I mean it's just so brown. It's like holding a baton of chocolate dreams, it's like the colour of nature! What colour would you call that?!' Dylan waxes lyrically on.

'Actually it's Pantone 17-1126,' Ashley adds, but that doesn't stop Dylan.

'I just had to have it, I just had to bring it back to show you guys. I just didn't notice all this nature stuff until now, but now I can't help seeing things that I didn't see before. Suddenly I'm spotting cats. I never really liked cats: now all I want to do is run after them and maybe bite their tails a bit. I have to say, I love this place!'

'Well this is just great, Dylan, I mean just great. I couldn't be more pleased,' I whimper. Just at that second, Dylan begins to sniff the air.

'Yummy! I can smell breakfast. I just need to, you know, go to the bathroom first. I can't see one. I'll just go by that tree!' Dylan says. She's just about to run off when I grab her.

'There's a toilet right there!'

'Oh right, yeah!' Dylan says, heading to the camp bathroom.

'Well I think it's fair to say that she's not any better.'

'It's just a stick. What is she talking about?'
Ashley says, still staring at the stick in her
hand. 'Maybe we could get someone on a
farm to adopt her. I mean I'm allergic to dogs
anyway,' Ashley says, blowing her nose.

'We can't do that, we've got to help
her,' I insist. 'Wait, are there mirrors in that
bathroom?'

'ARRRRRRGGGGGGGGGGGGGGGGH!' we hear
from inside.

SAUSAGES

Ashley and I burst into the toilets to see Dylan trembling in front of the mirror, hat in hand.

'I have ears, I HAVE EARS, I HAVE BIG FLOPPY HAIRY EARS!' Dylan sobs.

'Oh my word!' I say, taking a closer look. 'They're getting bigger!' I say, staring at them.

'What?' Dylan asks. 'What do you mean they're getting bigger! You knew about this?' Dylan turns and looks at me. 'I have ears and you didn't think to let me know? Just for the record if either of you turned into an animal, I'd tell you!'

'Well, I thought they might, you know, drop off.'

'Drop off?! They're ears. Ears don't drop off! Now, if I'd grown a couple of autumn leaves, I'd understand—but ears!'

'In Tyler's defence, we didn't want to alarm you. You might not take too well to discovering that you're basically no longer human,' Ashley adds.

'You knew too! What am I going to do?' Dylan asks, trying to swipe them off her head, but her hand just kept sliding straight through. 'Why won't they go?!'

'They're holograms. That's the good news,'
I say, taking a closer look, before running my
hand through them. It was like dipping my
fingers into a TV screen: I could feel a tingle
but nothing more. 'They're just holograms.
They must have fused from the phone when
you were playing with that app last night.'

'Oh, let me have a go,' Ashley says, waving her hands through them too.

'Will everyone stop wafting my ears!' Dylan yelps.

'Your ears?' Ashley confirms. 'You see, you quite like them,' she adds. 'Maybe it's not so bad, perhaps they'll grow on you.'

'By the size of them I'd say they already have,' I chuckle slightly.

'Ha, yes, that's very funny,' Ashley chuckles too.

'Do you two want to stop that now please, I'm really not in the mood for clever word play,' Dylan snarls, dancing around swiping at her ears like she's being attacked by an annoying wasp. 'Well, get rid of them! Use the phone to reverse the effects!' Dylan says, shaking her head violently as if the ears are going to just fly off.

'The phone broke last night.'

'Well, why do I still have dog ears then?' Dylan squeals.

'We're not sure, it's a real puzzler . . .' Ashley muses. 'In many ways, this is a really interesting scientific quandary.'

'I swear, one more word and I'll bite you!' Dylan squeals.

'Classic dog behaviour,' Ashley shrugs. 'Hey, maybe if we figure this out we could be like cybervets, travelling the globe helping cyberpets. They might even turn us into a comic. I'm talking about a franchise with action figures, movies, sequels, prequels, spin-offs, the lot,' Ashley says, getting quite excited.

'WHAT AM I SUPPOSED TO DO?' Dylan wails.

'We need to find a way to fix the phone. Until we can figure out how the hologram is powering itself we can't hope to reverse the effects,' I tell Dylan. 'It's probably best if you don't show anyone your doggy ears in the meantime.'

'Show anyone?! Who am I going to show?' Dylan asks, grabbing a towel that is hanging by the sink before laying on the floor and curling up like a sad little puppy.

'Can you just switch the transponder thingy and reverse the whatnots?' Dylan says, trying to find the words. 'No that's not right? I can't remember what I mean. I feel like I'm losing my mind . . . oh man, I wish I had a sausage . . .' Dylan sighs.

I look at Ashley, she looks back at me. Ashley gives me a look as if to say 'you need to tell her'.

'That's because you might be,' I say, patting her on the top of her head. 'Not losing your mind!' I hastily add. 'But you know, changing a bit. It's not just that you have dog ears. I think, *we* think,' I say, looking at Ashley, 'that you may be developing the personality of a dog too. You seem to be quite mutt-like in your behaviour,' I add, bracing myself for Dylan's reaction.

'What?' Dylan says looking surprised. 'No, I

just forgot the thing I was saying: that happens to people all the time,' she says, the panic in her voice clear for all to hear.

'People do, but not you, Dylan,' Ashley mutters quietly. '*You* never forget.'

It's very hard telling your friends that they're slowly becoming an animal before your very eyes. They tend not to believe you.

'That's not truuueeeeeeooooOOOWWwww!' Dylan howls.

'You see,' Ashley interrupts, 'that bit, the way you said "not truuuuuue" the end bit, well that was a bit like a dog howling. That sort of defeats your argument.'

'I did not howl!' Dylan barks.

'OK, that was a bit like a bark,' I say, trying to be nice but also fair.

'A bit howly and a bit barky,' Ashley says, shaking her head. 'Classic cyberdog.'

'I am not turning into a dog!' Dylan yells at us both, 'Well, apart from having dog ears, I'll give you that, they are very doggy, but as for the rest of it. No, you're making it up.'

'Look at yourself,' Ashley adds. 'You're lying on the floor next to the heater. Classic *Canis lupus familiaris*,' Ashley says.

'I am not behaving like an animal!' Dylan whines.

'You went for a run this morning, you keep talking about sausages, not to mention this!' I say, pulling the stick out of my pocket.

'Oh what, so can't a friend bring another friend a present any more without it being considered odd?' Dylan says, looking sad.

'It's not a present, Dylan, it's a big chewed stick! We don't give people sticks, whether they are friends or enemies,' I say, but Dylan's not listening: instead her eyes are following the stick as I gesticulate with it. 'Oh for goodness' sake!' I sigh, before throwing it across the room. Without blinking Dylan is up and is bounding on all fours before coming to a skidding halt. She grabs the stick in her mouth and hurtles back, dropping it by my feet. She looks up at me and smiles, as if she wants me to throw it again. For a second Dylan's lost in the moment before she cries out . . .

'Oh my word! I'm a dog! ARRRRGHOOOO-OOOOOOWWWWWWWWWW!' She lets out another pained howl.

'Whhhhhachoooooooo!' Ashley suddenly cries. 'Sorry, my allergies are playing up. I'm allergic to animals,' she says blowing her nose.

'Oh, this just gets better and better,' I sigh.

'Is this why I couldn't remember those words? Am I going to lose my nerd?' she asks, looking as if the world is about to end.

'At the current rate Dylan is changing, I think we've only got about 48 hours until . . .' Ashley says looking at us.

'Until what?' we both reply.

'Until we lose you forever, Dylan. Until your transformation from human to dog, even a holographic one, is complete.'

'Forever?' Dylan sobs.

'Until all that's left of your brain is a dog,

until you've turned into an animal for the rest of time. The only good thing is that dogs live until they're about 15, so you'll only have few years before death releases you from your torment,' Ashley says, dryly. 'Can I have your computer when you're gone?'

For a second Dylan says nothing, then a high-pitched whine starts.

'Don't worry, Dylan,' I say trying to reassure her, 'Ashley and I will help you out. We'll save you, won't we Ash?!' I say through my gritted teeth.

'Yes, we will give it our best. Considering the odds, the chances of getting caught, and the fact that we have no equipment with which to rebuild the phone, I say we have a 23.768%

chance of making it. But if the worst comes to the worst, one of us will keep you as a pet. Not me obviously, I'm allergic, but maybe Fitz, or a dog home or something.' At that the whining doubles in loudness.

'Ash!' I yell.

'Sorry, if it were me I'd want to know the odds,' Ashley says.

'Right we need a plan,' I say, trying take control of the situation and hopefully stop Ashley from making it any worse. 'No one is going to treat you any different, Dylan. You're our friend, not an animal. Right now we need to focus on how to fix this. So, what do we know?'

'The earth was formed from the Big Bang

'. . .' Ashley begins.

'About this situation!' I say, cutting across her.

'Of course, that would make sense,' Ashley nods.

'Well, there was a storm,' Dylan says.

'Good girl, have a biscuit,' I say, tossing her a snack.

'That would explain why the phone malfunctioned in the first place, but not what's powering Dylan's ears? Let's go through everything again. What else?'

'There was wind too, we had the phone, I was playing with it in the bathroom, hiding so no one would see. The moon was really bright.'

'The moon?' I say.

'Yes, the moon was out last night, I saw it when I came back early,' Dylan says.

'That's it!' Ashley and I both say. 'The phone is lunar powered, so the moon must be the source of the holographic ears.'

'Of course, the moon's about to be at its fullest,' Ashley says. 'It's the biggest and brightest one we've had for years. That would explain why the transformation is happening so quickly—the moon is just feeding the hologram and accelerating the transformation. That explains why it got worse overnight.'

'It's like plugging an electric guitar into an amp and turning up the volume. It's just going to get louder.'

'The moon might be weaker in a few days, but it might be too late by then,' Ashley says, looking at Dylan.

'Oh my, that's it, the full moon, the ears, doesn't that sound a bit werewolfy?'

'Can't I just stay away from the moon for a bit?' Dylan asks.

'Oh Dylan, your poor animal brain's not thinking right. The moon is around us all the time, even when we can't see it. Its gravity pulls the oceans and creates tides all day, everyday. Trying to run away from the moon is like trying to escape from air,' Ashley says stroking her chin. 'The only way to stop this is by reversing the hologram's effect, and for that . . .'

'We need to rebuild the phone, and reverse the effect using the Change Me! app,' I interrupt.

'It's our best hope,' Ashley agrees. 'If we don't do it soon, we might be too late and Dylan will be lost to the animal world forever.'

FRESH MEAT

I pull out the phone from my pocket and take the back off it. It's broken and bashed up, but before I get a chance to look at it properly it's snatched off me.

'No phones for you, you didn't earn enough Happy Points,' Pipper says, smiling. 'In fact, if I remember right, you're on minus seventy-five, which is some sort of record.' she grins.

'No!' I yell. 'Please, I need it back. Please let me have it, you don't understand!' I try and explain, but how do you explain you need to unturn your friend into a dog?

'Earn more Happy Points after breakfast!' she snaps, pointing towards the canteen.

We march into the breakfast canteen and head straight for our table. Thank goodness that we live in a society where people don't mix. There at the back of the canteen, is the Woodlouse table. 'Team meeting,' I announce. 'Let's head over there and work out a plan.'

'Are you OK, Dylan?' I say, turning around.

'Yes, I am not a dog, I am not a dog, I am not a dog . . .' she repeats over and over.

'Atta girl,' I say, before giving her another

biscuit. 'You need to try and hide this from everyone for now. You don't want them freaking out.'

'I know what you're up to!' I suddenly hear in my ear.

'Courtney. What a lovely surprise,' I say, spinning around doing my best fake grin.

'I know what's going on.'

'You do?' I say, nervously.

'I heard you,' she says. 'Talking about hiding.'

'You did?' I ask.

'Yes, I know what you're hiding from. From the monster—you must have heard the howling, we all did!'

I look at the other two. 'Howling?'

'Oh my, like the howling, we all heard it this morning, just like the one we heard last night.'

'Last night?' I say.

'I'm pretty sure the only explanation is that there is a werewolf on the loose. There literally can be no other explanation. I watch

a lot of TV so I'm very knowledgeable you
know,' Courtney snaps.

'Ha ha,' I try laughing it off. 'Werewolves . . . !'

'Will you stop saying everything I've just
said, it's getting very annoying. Do I need
to remind you that I'm here trying to relax?
I find it very hard to relax when you are just
repeating everything. I've been for a morning
yoga workout, I've had my aura cleansed,
and been at one with nature for a whole, like,
seven minutes trying to get over the stress.'

'Been at one with nature?' Ashley says,
looking at Courtney suspiciously.

'Again with the repeating. Yeah, it's like,
you know, emptying your head of everything.'

'And that took as long as seven minutes?'

I ask. I know we're trying not to draw attention to ourselves, but some opportunities are just too good to miss.

'I know you're insulting me, I don't know what that means, but I know you're being like totally rude and why oh why is the little one sniffing my leg!' she snaps at Dylan.

'Sorry, you just smell of the lake, lovely lake,' Dylan says, looking up at Courtney.

'How did you know I've been to the lake?' she asks, looking perplexed. Just as I think she may be on to us, who should appear but Blane.

'Hey Courtney, why are you hanging around with these guys?' he says coming over and joining in.

'Oh, are you guys back together?' I say trying to change the subject.

'Yeah, like totally,' he says. Honestly, if someone else uses the word 'like' again, I think I may well scream my lungs out.

'Yeah, it turns out the different things I wanted, after talking to Courtney I didn't want them after all.'

'Blane, please don't talk to them about us.

Us is between just me and you, about six of my besties, my twitter feed, and my Instagram peeps, you know, like, it's totally private,' Courtney says, shutting him down. 'And, please don't engage with their leader, she might try and kiss you again.'

'Can't people pretend to be football players in order to illicitly gain a DNA sample and stop someone's arm growing three feet long spontaneously without people assuming it's romantic?' I ask.

'It's the oldest trick in the book,' Courtney shrugs.

'Also, we don't have a leader,' Ashley pipes up. 'We are, if anything, a fluid collective of like-minded individuals. An equal collective.

A post-revolutionary union. Freedom fighters, with knowledge as our weapon, and truth as our cause.'

'That literally made no sense at all,' Courtney huffs. 'Just stay away from all the good hiding places, because if this thing comes back, I simply refuse to be eaten. It should be one of you lesser people. I have over fifteen thousand Instagram followers relying on me to brighten their day. I can't be, like, dying. People won't survive without me.'

'I'm sure it was just a raccoon or something,' I say, trying to throw her off the scent.

'That was no raccoon,' says Blane. 'These woods are haunted. They say that a werewolf stalks these hills. There's this kid in the Fox cabin, who knows someone whose grandfather knows a guy who once saw something spooky in these hills, probably ages ago. Everyone's talking about it—what more evidence do you want? It must be true. Anyway, I'm off to play some ball to take my mind off this whole ordeal,' he says, throwing a ball up with one hand and catching it with the other.

'Ball?' Dylan perks up. 'Man, that's a good ball, I bet you could really throw that far, you know, for someone to chase!' Dylan says, staring at the ball, not letting it escape her gaze. 'Boy, that looks like a tasty ball, all leathery and delicious. Smells good enough to eat. Throw me the ball Blane, please? If you throw me the ball I will bring it back, maybe I could lick your face, and then we could throw it all over again, just maybe do that for an hour or so? What do you say master, can I call you that?'

'Master? You're right, the little one is the weirdest,' Blane says to Courtney.

'Call off your minions, Fitz, no one is going to lick anyone's face,' Courtney snaps.

'Dylan is just joking, you know, ha ha ha. Anyway, werewolves aren't real, it was probably something to do with the storm,' I say, adding a voice of reason to the debate.

'How do you know? Have you ever seen one?' Courtney asks.

'Well no. No one has . . .'

'Well how do you know then if you haven't seen one?'

'Well, by not seeing one, that's how I know they're not real,' I say trying to work out Courtney's logic.

'You can't say they're not real until you actually see one,' Courtney smiles confidently.

'Wait . . . errr,' Ashley mumbles, 'you can't say something's not real until you've seen it? What . . . I . . .'

'But . . . eh . . .' I stutter.

'Like, obviously. Considering you lot are supposed to be clever, you're, like, buffering like a TV special with slow WiFi,' Courtney says. 'I'm bored of you. Let's go Blane, I need a mango and elderflower fruit latte with ginseng,' Courtney says, wandering off. 'Can I use the Change Me! app on you, Blane? I need to give my Insta-sisters something to keep them happy for the day.'

'But what about the ball . . . ?' Blane says sadly.

'Blane, remember what we said, we want the same things now, I want to go this way, so therefore you do too. Do you need to see the diagram again . . .' Courtney says, pulling out a piece of paper with an arrow on it and a message saying, 'I'm going this way, you are too.'

'Oh man,' Blane says turning and throwing the ball out of the canteen door. 'But I don't want to have my picture taken with doggy ears.'

'BALL!' Dylan yells running after it.

'For the last time,' Courtney says, pulling him along like a stroppy toddler, 'they are not dog ears, they are wolf ears, the app turns you into a wolf, Blane. It's topical, you know, because of the werewolf thing. Hashtag pray for Courtney, you know, because of all the danger I might be in. Keep up Blane . . .'

Ashley and I look at each other. 'Did she just say . . .?'

'Yep,' Ashley says sternly.

'And if we don't change Dylan back, she won't be just a cute dog then . . .?' I ask.

'No, at some point she'll change from dog to wolf.'

'BALL!' Dylan says, returning with the ball in her mouth, the leather sinking between her hungry teeth, her nose twitching and quivering, and a wild look in her eye. Those were the signs Mr Jones had warned us about in Myths and Legends class.

'Agh!' I cry in fear.

'Where's Blane?' Dylan says, looking around for her playmate.

'He's gone, erm, who's for breakfast . . .' I stumble. 'That's what we should do, get some breakfast!' I smile.

'Oh yes, let's. I'm in the mood for meat, just some meat really, you know like a really rare steak, you know, all juicy and bloody,' Dylan says, beginning to drool.

'What about some fruit?' Ashley says, trying not to look scared. 'Fruit's good too.'

'Nah, I'm just in the mood for meat, really fresh meat.'

'How fresh? Not too fresh?' I say, backing away. 'You know, not like "alive" fresh?' I ask.

I look at Ashley, she looks at me. Well this is great—not only is our best friend an animal, but she may well want to eat me too.

MIDNIGHT HIKE

We make our way over to the Woodlouse table
having first grabbed a few slices of bacon to
keep Dylan from nibbling on one of us. I look
at her as she begins to eat. It's kind of strange
to see someone, knowing that they're on their
way to becoming a werewolf. Suddenly you
feel like you're one of those people on a nature
documentary, observing animal behaviour. The
camp is up and awake now, children from all

over are drifting in to get their fill before the day's activities start. Speaking of which, what are we doing today? I look around, and there written on the board is a list of the day's fun, like "specials" in an awful restaurant. There's a fire building and maintenance workshop, a woodland wildlife seminar, water volleyball, the usual fare—horrible, but all stuff I can cope with—and then I see it. The words fill me with dread: "Midnight Hike". I look outside. The sky is clear and cloudless. The hike tonight will be under a full moon. I look over at Dylan, her face now licking the plate of bacon around the table like an animal. Is it me or do her teeth look pointier than before?

'Have you seen the news?' Ashley says,

nodding to the board.

'I know!' I whisper. 'This is going to be a disaster!'

'What's a disaster?' Peggy says, taking a seat next to me.

'Oh, you know, just looking at the midnight hike, it just isn't my cup of tea,' I say.

'Because of the werewolf?' she says.

'Surely you don't believe in all that?' Ashley asks, trying to gauge whether telling Peggy would be a good idea or not.

'Nope, but if it gets us out of a midnight hike, I'm all for it!' she grins.

'Oh,' I say. 'But if one really did want to get out of a midnight hike, how would one do that?' I ask, looking at Dylan, who's now licking

the bacon fat off her
nose with her tongue, or
trying to at least.

'One would have
to have broken both legs,
probably, either that or terrible weather, so you
could try a rain dance I suppose. Although,
they're very strict about everyone doing all
events. They have waterproofs . . .' Peggy says
ominously, 'and they're not afraid to use them.'

'I think it's time to get my phone back,'
I say. 'Who's for a spot of breaking and
entering . . .?'

'You know,' Ashley begins, 'as much as I'm
grateful that you appeared in our lives, I have
to say things were far less illegal before you

moved to Happyville, Fitz.'

'Well look at it this way, it's good training for the end of days,' I reply.

Ten minutes later we are all outside Pipper's office. It's one of the many log cabins nestled in the woods. The outside is decorated with paintings of pastel flowers, and woodland creatures, and there's a pink door with a sign above it that reads: 'A smile costs nothing!'. The building couldn't be more Pipper if it tried.

'OK, Operation "Break into Pipper's office and go and get the phone without her noticing": so let's do that shall we then . . .' I trail off. 'OK, we'll decide on the name later,'

I say, still trying to grapple with my new role as undercover geek person. 'We need a plan.'

'What about Dylan staying here outside,' Ashley says. 'Guarding the place, keeping an eye out, letting us know with a succession of loud noises.'

'You mean as a guard dog don't you?' Dylan says looking miffed.

'Well . . . yes,' Ashley says. 'Look if I was part cat and you needed some balls of wool playing with, I'd be right there for you.' Ashley shrugs.

'Do you want me to woof?' Dylan says, looking indignant.

'No, no,' I add, 'I think that would give the game away. Just a cough will do.'

'Fine, I'll do that,' Dylan sighs, before sitting back on her legs and putting her arms in front, exactly how a dog would sit.

'Right, so I say we kick the door down,' Ashley says, flexing her limbs. 'It's a shame there isn't a storm. I could use my leg like a combine harvester of devastation, you know; tear the door off its hinges. Still, this is war, it calls for all sorts of sacrifices,' she says, taking a run-up.

'WAIT!' I cry. 'Or we could just open it,' I say, looking around making sure that no one is watching before pushing on the handle.

'Well, where's the fun in that. You promised me breaking *and* entering!' Ashley says, disappointedly.

'Well, if you're good, maybe you could give the door a quick elbow on the way out,' I say, as we go through.

The cabin is quiet and dark, full of fluffy things like toy animals and tiny novelty trolls impaled on pencils. The first thing that hit us is the smell.

'Holy macaroni!' Ashley says, covering her nose. 'What is that?!'

'I think it's her scented oils collection,' I say, spotting the many air fresheners around the room, along with flowers and scented candles.

'It smells like a unicorn guffed a rainbow in here,' Ashley says, gagging on the sweet floral odour.

'I know, it's sickening, but keep it together. Look, her desk,' I say, pointing to the corner.

'She's the neatest person in the world. I bet she's got a lost property drawer for all manner of things she's confiscated over the years. Probably the left one, as she's right-handed, and the drawer on the right would be more useful for admin stuff,' I say.

Ashley goes over and opens the left-hand drawer and pulls out a box of phones. 'You're good. I'm thinking of inviting you back into my army,' Ashley grins. 'Here it is!' she says, grabbing the hologram phone. 'Oh look, there's other old handsets we can use for components too,' she says, popping them into her rucksack.

'Let's . . .' but I don't have time to say the word 'go' before we hear coughing from outside. I look at Ashley, she looks back at me.

It's Dylan. Our cover has been blown. Ashley slams the drawer shut and pops her rucksack back on her shoulders and we run to the door, falling through it just in time to see Pipper and Courtney coming round the corner. The door shuts behind us just as they catch our eyes. We made it, just.

'Oh really, you three again?!' Courtney says. 'Are you following me?'

'How can we be following you, you're walking towards us,' I say, trying not to antagonize her, but really, she's old enough to know how following someone works!

'Well, what *are* you doing here girls?' asks Pipper.

'We were just wondering if you had any

books on myths and legends, you know, we wanted to catch up with some school work,' I blurt out, saying the first thing that pops into my head.

'Memo to the dork squad!' Courtney sighs. 'We're not at school, you're not supposed to do any learning when you're not there! It's, like, the law!' Courtney says, amazed by our audacity.

'I know, but I was really interested in what you were saying earlier,' I smile.

'What's this, Courtney?' Pipper asks.

'Basically, I'm, like, the cleverest person. I know about things like vampires and werewolves and stuff,' Courtney says, showing off to Pipper. 'I've watched loads of books and

TV about all this sort of stuff,' she grins.

'Oh yeah?' I say, playing along. I look over at Dylan, who is busy trying to chase a butterfly through the undergrowth.

'Well, when it comes to werewolves, and that's what we're dealing with here, the only way to catch them is to offer up some sort of human sacrifice. That's what they're after, they like to eat people. If you can find someone willing to die, then catching a werewolf is easy. All you need to do is surround the said werewolf and take it down. The death has to be instant though, like a silver bullet through the noggin, a spike through the heart, or a just a general chopping off of the head should work too,'

Courtney says, with a skip in her voice.

'A human sacrifice?' Ashley gulps.

'Oh yes, werewolves like to attack people they know, like a family member or a friend, someone they have a connection with, it's their thing. And once they've eaten their first human, there's no going back. Why are you asking about werewolves anyway? Did you hear the howling too?! I knew you did, you think that there's a werewolf around as well. Maybe I turned my back on monster hunting too soon!' Courtney snaps.

'Werewolves? What are you guys talking about?' Pipper asks.

'Let me tell you all about it,' Courtney says. 'Our story starts with a beautiful maiden and some spooky woods . . .' she says, wandering off with Pipper towards the campfire.

(((◯

The next six hours are spent trying to keep Dylan away from everyone during camp activities. All I want to do is fix the phone before the moon comes out, but it's hard to do when you're up to your ears in friendship bracelets and falafel sculpting. I'm not proud of myself, but at one point I did do a small rain dance when no one was watching. It did no good—all I got was a little mist, not enough to cancel the hike, but at least it's hidden the moon for now. We all line up, we have maps, head torches, and whistles (for emergencies only) in case we get lost. The entire camp is celebrating this by blowing whistles constantly, therefore making them completely useless.

'How are you feeling, Dylan?' I ask her. She's been giddy with excitement for hours. She's dying for a walk. Fortunately the mist has descended, meaning that the moon has disappeared, at least for the moment.

'I'm ready,' Ashley says, lining up outside with a couple of bags in her hand.

'What are they for?' I ask.

'You can get fined if you don't pick up after your pet,' she says.

'Oh right, good thinking,' I say.

'I mean, I really hope it doesn't come to that. I think our friendship will have crossed a line, but I also don't want to get a fine.'

We file out into the woods. Ashley and I hang back. We manage to keep Dylan with us—she's busy sniffing everything, the air, the plants, a big puddle.

'How are you feeling Dylan? Well done on keeping your hat on all day.'

'Thanks, I like hats. I feel fine. Everything smells so amazing. It's like suddenly discovering a million new colours at once. I can smell where you've been, I can smell who was here an hour ago. I can smell . . .'

'Please stop saying the word smell,' Ashley interrupts. 'I will pay you to stop saying it.'

'You've never been a dog person have you Ashley? All I've ever done is been a faithful friend, love you, bring you sticks. Why won't you let me love you?' Dylan pines.

'Just relax everyone, we've only got another hour of this and then it'll be over, we can head back to the cabin and get working on that phone,' I say to Dylan.

'Yeah, OK, or well, you know, whatever,' she says. Ashley looks at me.

'What do you mean "whatever"?' Ashley asks.

'I was just thinking, it might not be the worst thing in the world to stay like this. I'm happy, I'm getting fresh air, my new nose can sme . . . I have a great new nose,' Dylan says.

'Dylan, you can't become a full-time holographic dog,' I say. 'People will notice.'

'What's wrong with dogs? Everyone likes a

cute dog. I can just be that person: you know, there's always someone who's double-jointed and they can bend their thumbs back in weird ways, or the kid who can do that thing where they turn their eyelids inside out. Well, I can be the person who's a puppy,' she says, smiling. She has no idea that she's not a puppy but a wolf, a man-eating werewolf. I saw the way she was eyeing my ears at lunch, looking at them like they were a couple of pork chops.

'Let's just try and fix the phone,' I say, 'and take it from there.'

'Well OK,' Dylan says. 'Oooo, I can smell a rabbit!' she yelps, following the scent with her nose.

'Do we tell her?' Ashley asks me quietly.

'That she's not a puppy, but a killer!'

'I think she's had a quite a lot of news today, let's save some fun for tomorrow,' I suggest. 'Besides which, I think we have more to worry about,' I say, looking up at the mist. The clouds are getting thicker now, they are beginning to drift and float away as the light breeze blows in. I can see it, nestling behind the thick cloud, the bright circle of the moon.

'I think we might be in trouble,' Ashley says, looking up at the sky. 'Dylan, stay close.'

'Dylan?' I say turning round, but she's not there. She's gone.

HOWLING
AT THE MOON

Ashley and I sprint through the undergrowth
like a couple of gazelles—gazelles in pain.
Why is the outdoors so prickly?

'Ouch! Are you sure she went this way?' I
cry to Ashley, who's bounding ahead of me.

'I think so. The last thing she said was she
smelt a rabbit. This is perfect rabbit country—
just look at the ground.'

'How do you know?' I ask.

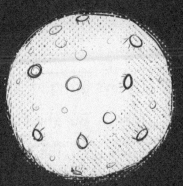

'I guess some of that woodland wildlife seminar went in,' she says, shrugging.

After what feels like miles we end up at a clearing. The trees are gone, there's just a hill in the distance with the moon behind. The clouds have completely disappeared, the moon is huge and bright, like the old spotlights they used to shine at skyscrapers years ago. We look around.

'DYLAN!' I cry out. Suddenly we see a shadow. Someone's climbing to the top of the hill—it's her, it must be her. 'DYLAN!!' I yell again. Her shadowy silhouette turns to face us. For a moment I think it's all going to be OK,

Dylan's going to come back to us, back to her friends. But she quickly turns away again and looks up to the moon. She crouches down low, and then I can see her looking at her hands, next she rips off her hat and her ears begin to grow, and even though she's far away I can see her body jolt and shake like she's not in control of it. Then, from nowhere, she lets out an almighty howl. It echoes through the woods and valley taking my breath away. A moment later, she's off, running into the wilderness. Dylan is gone. I look at Ashley, but there's no time to say anything, I can hear a chorus of emergency whistles as the rest of the camp run towards us.

'Did you hear that?' Peggy yells. She's the first to arrive, followed by Herbert who screams.

'DID YOU SEE IT? THE WEREWOLF, DID YOU? YOU MUST HAVE HEARD IT, EVEN I HEARD IT!'

'I heard it,' I say looking over, but now I'm surrounded by other kids all asking me questions at once.

'I don't think it's safe out here,' Herbert whimpers.

'For once the little dweeb is right,' Courtney says, fighting her way through the crowds. 'Everyone back to camp, I'm calling an emergency meeting.'

'What do we do?' I say turning to Ashley, 'Dylan's out there somewhere.'

'I don't knoooooowwwwhhhhooooccccchoooo!' Ashley sneezes.

'We need . . . wait, did you just sneeze?' I ask.

'DYLAN!' We both shout out. We break off the path as everyone files past us, and head out into the woods on our own, the moon like a torch showing us the way.

'She must be close, if your sinuses are playing up,' I cry in delight.

'Thank goodness for a poorly constructed immune system!' Ashley grins.

I look around, but I can't see a thing, it's so dark and the shadows from the trees begin to play tricks on my eyes. It seems everywhere I look I see shadows moving, wolves in every direction, but as soon as I turn, they're gone.

'Whhhhaaaaaaaa . . .' Ashley starts

before losing her sneeze again.

'You can be our Dylan detector,' I say, grabbing her and spinning her round slowly. Then, as I turn her seventy-five degrees to the west, she lets out an enormous sneeze. It works! We walk in the direction she's pointing and I fan Ashley out like a metal detector looking for treasure. A sneeze here, and we change direction slightly. A sneeze there, and we correct our course.

'What if she eats us?' Ashley says, suddenly aware that she's leading the way.

'She probably won't, I mean she likes us,' I say, trying to calm her down.

'Probably won't?' Ashley says. 'You heard what Courtney said about how werewolves go for people they know!' Ashley squeals.

'Oh what does Courtney know about anything,' I try to reassure her. 'Although she was right about there being a werewolf on the loose,' I mumble. Just at that second Ashley lets out a huge sneeze.

'We're close,' I say, coming to a halt.

'Hey guys!!' comes the familiar voice of Dylan. 'You will not guess what some people just leave lying around.'

'Torch!' I say to Ashley. She quickly grabs it from her backpack. Ashley shines it towards Dylan's voice and there she is, not three feet away, gnawing on a huge bone.

'I mean it's just so wasteful? Wanna bite?' she offers. Ashley and I say nothing. Dylan is sat munching on the bone, her ears are enormous now, her eyes are bright blue but icy cold, her fingers are long and hairy, with huge claws hanging off the ends, her nose is black and shiny, and behind her a scraggly tail wags menacingly. A huge pink tongue hangs from her open mouth. But by far the worst thing is her pointed teeth, tearing and picking at the bone, like precise, ivory pliers. Like they could pull apart anything and anyone on a moment's whim. She is a wolf—she is the most werewolfish thing I've ever seen.

'Why are you all staring at me?' she says.

'You know, you've got a thing just there?' Ashley says pointing at her cheek. Dylan wipes herself clean.

'Has it gone?' she asks.

'No, it's still there. I think it's a whisker. You have whiskers, Dylan. And a tail. A MASSIVE TAIL!!!' Ashley wails.

'Hey, I know Ashley, I know . . .' she says, trying to calm Ashley down. 'The last thing I remember is smelling that rabbit, then nothing. I woke up on the hill. I couldn't see you guys, so I came back, I smelt the way home, that's when I saw,' she said, looking at her swishing tail. 'I'm not a dog am I? I'm not a cute puppy any more. I'm a wolf,' she smiles.

We both nod.

'I thought sooooooooooOOOoooo,' she half howls. 'Well, I came to say goodbye,' Dylan says, finishing her bone.

'What?' I say. 'Goodbye? Dylan, you can't go. Just come back to the camp and we can fix this. You won't be safe out there!' I say.

'I'll be safer out there than I am in here,' she says. 'I knooooOOOOOOoooow what this place is like. If I go back there Courtney will have me killed, stuffed, and mounted on the wall. Plus I've got this whoooOOOOOooooole howl thing going on now. I may or may not end up eating a few kids,' Dylan smiles, and her fangs flash in the torchlight.

'Yes,' Ashley says. 'It's true,' she nods.

'Ashley!' I yell, 'do you want her to go?!'

'No, but I don't want her to get hurt even more,' Ashley says, looking sad.

'So this really is goodbye then?' I say.

We haven't even rebuilt the phone yet, how are we going to fix her in time? I grab the phone from Ashley's backpack and shine Ashley's torch on the phone as I pull the back off. It's a mess, a broken mess of wires and burnt out components. The battery is a wreck, the wires are probably fixable, but where are we going to find a soldering iron out here. Perhaps Dylan is right after all. Maybe it's hopeless. Maybe the fight has been lost already. Suddenly the moment is broken by the sounds of voices, as kids start milling around the camp preparing for the hunt. Dylan begins to sniff the air wildly.

'There are too many people around here, I need to gooooOOOOoooooo,' she says, giving us a smile, before looking out into the miles of black empty forest. And then, with a single spring, she's gone, disappearing into the woods. Is that it, will we ever see her again? I don't know, but I'm not going to give up hope.

I turn to Ashley. 'There's still time to save her.'

'It's over,' Ashley sighs, sitting down.

'What are we going to tell her parents? Will they even notice?'

Ashley shrugs. 'What have we done?' she whimpers.

'It was no one's fault,' I say, trying to

comfort her. Ashley looks up at me. 'Well, all right, some of it is my fault? Listen, while there's at least a theoretical possibility that we can get her back we should try. Yes, she's off in the woods. Yes, she's safe there for the time being. But, if we can lure her back, get the phone fixed, and reverse the transformation, we might be able to get Dylan back forever.'

'Yes, or she may eat us.'

'Yes, that is a possibility too, but I'd like to think if the same thing happened to me, you and Dylan would do everything to help me,' I say. 'You know . . . like comrades . . . in a war . . . this is a bit like a war. I know you'd have my back when the robots come for us. If you think about it, Pipper, Kipper, and Courtney are like the robots . . .' I carry on.

'OK, OK,' Ashley says. 'Please stop, this is tortuous. I'll help, just end the metaphor. But how are we going to fix the phone? We need help. We're going to have to scour the camp for whatever we can find. But to get everything we need, we're going to need help, we're going to need soldiers, the best of the best.' Ashley smiles.

MEAT SUIT

We head back to the camp. It's abuzz with panic and intrigue. Just at that second, Courtney bursts through a crowd of campers. She appears to be wearing a full ninja outfit.

'Fear not, kind village folk,' Courtney yells out, like she's a character from a fairy tale. 'I am brave Courtney, vampire slayer, werewolf neutralizer, and all round supernatural kick-asser,' she announces to huge cheers. 'I am here to save you. Just think that in years to come they will tell stories about this day. If we're lucky they may well turn this into a movie franchise, complete with merchandising options and a spin-off series too. I have already contacted several producers about this and I'm making enquiries with a talent agent. But, in the meantime, we need to bring this beast to account. We need to slay this monster! Who's with me!'

The campers let out a cheer and start grabbing whatever they can, to use as weapons.

'Are we all here?' Courtney asks. 'Where's

the third one? I forget her name, is it Dave?'
Courtney says, looking over at Ashley and me.

'She's called Dylan and she's . . . popped
out,' I say.

'Oh who cares, over to you our fearless
leader, Big Squirrel!'

'Good evening Happy Campers!' Big
Squirrel Kipper yells. 'Tonight was a bit of an
unexpected twist, but I think we all need to
calm down.'

'Thank goodness,' I whisper to myself.

'We have been hearing reports that
there is a werewolf on the loose in and
around the woods, but as we know
werewolves are not real . . .'

'At last, a sensible take on things,' I mutter.

'Well, that was until we all witnessed tonight's events. I mean, what more evidence do we need that a foul and killer beast roams these woods? We need to get properly armed. I'm talking pitchforks and silver bullets . . .'

'Oh for goodness' sake,' I blurt out. Everyone turns round and stares at me. 'Sorry, I didn't mean to blurt out . . . Actually, no, I'm not sorry. Pitchforks? Silver bullets? I mean isn't that a bit over the top? I mean, everyone knows werewolves aren't real? I'm not denying we all heard something terrifying, but there's no proof that it was a wolf. It could have been an angry badger, or a grumpy weasel,' I say, looking around hopefully to see if anyone's agreeing with me. No one is. No one is agreeing with me.

'Are you saying that we know everything about the world, everything there is to know?' Pipper asks.

'No,' I shrug. 'But we know enough to know that there aren't any werewolves. That goes for Loch Ness monsters, leprechauns, and wizards too. They're not real.'

'Oh, here she goes again,' Courtney sighs. 'Let me take over Big Squirrel. Are you saying that there isn't a beast out there, a half-human, half-dog who gets more powerful whenever the moon comes out?' Courtney asks.

'Well . . .' I start, then I think about Dylan, my half-human lunar-wolf. '. . . all I'm saying is that I don't think we've got anything to be scared of. If anything, we're the killers here. I mean, look at yourselves, reaching for whatever weapons you can find. Who are the real dangerous animals here, a lone werewolf, or us . . .' I say, leaving the profound thought hanging in the air.

'I will give one thousand pounds to anyone who captures and kills the beast!' Courtney suddenly yells. 'As you know, I am a girl of means and popularity. I've been voted most popular raccoon five times in a row in this camp, and I am literally too pretty to die. I will offer cash to anyone who brings me the beast . . . AND a part in the inevitable movie franchise!' she yells.

Pipper and Kipper look at each other and then high five! 'Let's do-o-o-o-o-o this!' they say. The whole room erupts into cheers.

'We leave on a wolf hunt in an hour!' Courtney says triumphantly.

'An hour gives us a head start, we need to find her first,' I say to Ashley, dragging her away from the crowd and back towards the woods.

'While we still have time, I'm not going to give up. Let's go and find the best of the best.'

We burst into Woodlouse cabin. 'Really? These guys? I mean, look at them,' Ashley says, looking over at the Woodlouse campers.

'Not so much the "best of the best" but the best of what we've got? We've only got a matter of minutes until we lose a Dylan and gain a very big dog.'

What I see is an army, ready and willing to help. They're preparing for a war, gathering weapons, getting ready to destroy poor Dylan. What they need is a leader, to make them see sense, to show them right from wrong.

'HAS ANYONE SEEN MY ATHLETE'S FOOT CREAM?' Herbert yells.

'Here, borrow mine,' Peggy offers.

'Really, these guys?' Ashley's eyes widen.

'Right, guys, I've got something to ask you,' I say, holding up the phone. 'Now, I know we're not officially allowed phones, but this is an emergency. I need your help. I need you to help me fix this. Here's a list of everything we need. Peggy, you said that you could get me a tin of soup the other day, can you still do that?'

'Yes,' Peggy says looking confused. 'Are

you really so desperate for something to read?' she asks.

'No, but I need the aluminum for a spot of electrical jiggery-pokery. If we can get the can, and everything else on the list, we'll be able to fix my phone and save someone's life,' I say looking around the cabin. 'Who's with me?'

'WHOSE LIFE WILL YOU SAVE?' Herbert asks.

'Dylan's,' I tell everyone. There are gasps from around the room.

'What?' Peggy asks. 'Is she in danger? Has the werewolf got her?'

'Yes, well sort of,' I say. There are cries of anguish and shock. 'But it's a little more complicated than that,' I say, trying to get quiet. 'Dylan is the werewolf.'

'Dun-Dun-DUUUN!' Ashley says making a dramatic musical sound effect. 'Sorry, it just felt like a "dun-dun-duuun" moment.'

'DYLAN'S THE WEREWOLF!' Herbert yells. Bearing in mind he's been yelling the whole time, this is extreme yelling.

'Yes, listen, I know what you're all thinking, but this was my fault. She was playing with the Change Me! app on my hologram phone and it turned her into a wolf, and because the hologram is lunar powered the transformation is being accelerated by the moon. But, if we can fix the phone, maybe we can reverse the effects and we can return Dylan back to normal, or as normal as she ever was. Now who's with me?'

'BUT WE COULD GET A THOUSAND DOLLARS IF WE KILL HER!' someone at the back yells excitedly.

'STOP!' Peggy yells. 'Dylan may be a bit different, but we are all different here, that's what makes us special . . .' Peggy turns to Herbert. 'Did we shun you just because you have nine toes? No, we embrace you, we help you. We were there when you put on your first pair of flip-flops.'

'That's a tough break, Herbert,' Ashley chips in.

'YES, but the point is that we are all different, we all have things that make other people frightened or judge us,' I say. 'With Dylan, she is just mostly a wild animal. Yes, she wants to eat us a bit, but that doesn't mean that we shouldn't help her. Yes, she's roaming the hills and howling at the moon, but is that a howl really a cry for help?' I ask.

'I think we can fix her,' Ashley joins in, 'but we're going to need your help.'

'So will you help us?' I ask. There's a murmur and a few sideways glances.

'YES!' Herbert shouts.

'Great,' I say. 'I want you to go out into that camp and find everything on this list: it has everything we need on it to fix the phone, and Herbert, you can be in charge of finding something to lure Dylan out of the woods with.

'YES!' Herbert shouts, nodding proudly.

'All those assault courses, all that forest

craft, it's all been leading up to this moment. This is our time, we are Woodlice and what do Woodlice do? They sneak, they slither, they go around not getting noticed. Can you do it, can you?! Go forth and become the Woodlice you were born to be!'

And with that they are gone, scurrying off on their secret mission to scavenge everything we need to fix my phone and save Dylan.

We rendezvous a short while later with a bag of swag, copper wire, metals of every kind, and old batteries.

'Where did you get all this stuff from?' I say, checking we have everything.

'Let's put it this way,' Peggy winks. 'The

falafel-maker will be out of action for a while.'

'Ha!' I say.

'You know, because we dismantled it,' Peggy adds.

'Yes I get it,' I say.

'Oh right, of course,' Peggy adds. 'I'm really bad at snappy banter.'

'It's been a learning curve for everyone,' I say helpfully.

I grab everything we're going to need and start work. I'm using old bed sheets as surgical gowns and a bunk as an operating table. In an ideal world a phone should be built in a sterile place, like a hospital theatre, away from particles and dust. When you're talking about components this small, a grain of dust is like a giant boulder within the engine.

'Are we ready to begin?' I ask Ashley.

'Ready, Fitz,' she replies.

'Screwdriver!' I hold out my hand and Ashley passes me the tiniest of all the screwdrivers, before mopping my brow. Luckily, she carries almost every tool imaginable in that backpack of hers.

I turn over the phone and slowly unscrew the back, wincing with pain as I look inside. 'It's bad, pretty bad, but I think we can fix this,' I say. 'A little music maestro,' I say and with that Ashley pulls out an iPod and mini speaker set from her bag.

'A little Debussy?' she asks.

'Perfect,' I say and with that we're away.

'I'm going to need the mercury, and those lithium batteries.' I take out the burned out battery and gently unpack one of the scavenged batteries from its box, like it's a new heart being given to a sick patient. Slowly, I lower the new battery in, and the phone instantly lights up. It's a small but significant victory. 'Soldering iron,' I ask. Ashley obliges once more. I fire it up and begin the slow and painful process of repairing the blown out components. 'Wait, something's not right, the motherboard's overheating, the power is too much. Scalpel!' I cry, 'I'm going to have to cut the wire.'

'No Fitz, it'll never work!' Ashley says. 'It's suicide!'

'This is my call, we do it my way or say goodbye to this operation here and now.'

'But what about the rules!' Ashley cries. 'You should never just cut the wire.'

'Rules, I laugh in the face of rules, I make my own up and play by no one else's,' I say. 'But if you're not with me, Ashley, then I may as well end the whole thing now. I need you by my side on this one,' I bark at her.

'Then do it!' she says passing me the scalpel.

I cut the wire, the overheating has stopped but we're losing power. 'We're losing her!' I say watching the phone's light fade. 'Wait, I've got an idea, give me another battery!' Ashley hands me one. I hook it up to a couple of wires.

'Stand clear!' I shout, before connecting the wires to the phone's battery. There's a spark then the lights of the phone come back up. We have power! Over the next few minutes or so I painstakingly fix the remainder of the phone until it's working again. It's a little delicate, but it seems to be holding for now. The lunar power pads are connected—any holographic jiggery-pokery won't work without the moon's power. I tear off my bedsheet gown and sit down in relief.

'Now, I wonder what Herbert's come up with to lure—' but before I can finish, he bursts through the cabin door covered head-to-toe in sausages.

'THAT'S RIGHT, WE MADE A SAUSAGE

SUIT!' Herbert yells in delight.

'What, how, why?!' I say. 'In fact, forget the rest, let's start with why?!'

'WELL, WE NEEDED TO FIND A WAY TO LURE DYLAN TO THE PHONE, RIGHT? SO I THOUGHT ABOUT WHAT DYLAN REALLY LIKES; SAUSAGES. ALL DOGS LIKE SAUSAGES. SO, HOW DO WE LURE SOMEONE WITH A SAUSAGE? WELL, WE MAKE THE SAUSAGE MOVE. AND AFTER SEVERAL ATTEMPTS TO PUT SKATEBOARD WHEELS ON A SAUSAGE, IT SOON BECAME CLEAR THAT MAKING A HUMAN SAUSAGE

SUIT WAS THE ONLY ANSWER!' Herbert yells.

'Is it me, or did that make perfect sense?' Ashley says, looking around.

Just at that second, we hear a noise, but it's not a howl. It's more like a screech, the screech of an angry cheerleader.

'YOU MIGHT WANT TO GET ON WITH IT. I THINK COURTNEY MAY HAVE SEEN US.' Herbert bellows.

'Oh great!' I cry, looking out of the window at the advancing mob. 'I know it goes against everything we believe, Woodlice, but

RUN!'

TAILS
OF THE
UNEXPECTED

'IT ALL MAKES SENSE NOW. SHE WAS THE ONLY ONE NOT THERE!' Courtney yells, striding up to our cabin. Normal kids don't say hello by sniffing butts! Dylan's the werewolf and they've been hiding her!' Courtney screams.

'I think, I THINK she might be onto us! Everyone run!' Ashley shouts, as we head into the trees. I look behind me to see Courtney, Blane, Pipper, and Kipper chasing us.

'Follow those NERDS!' Courtney yells, pointing after us. We duck between the bushes trying desperately to lose the crowd. I look behind me to see what looks like every kid chasing us. They have the smell of a reward in their noses, and Hollywood in their sights. The campers are carrying whatever weapons they've managed to get hold of: tennis rackets, oars from the boats, someone has even brought a courgette from the kitchen, which while it looks impressive isn't really going to do a lot of damage. As I'm running the moon comes out from behind the clouds again, and I can feel the phone light up and vibrate. I don't think it'll last long with the power of the moon surging into it, it may well blow up again. Hopefully, it'll last long enough to use on Dylan. Further and further we head out, Herbert dressed head-to-toe in pork products leading the way.

'Wow, imagine how fast he'd be with ten toes!' I say to Ashley.

'I know!' she agrees. 'Whachooooo!'

'We're close,' I say, panting for breath. We come to a clearing and take a second. Suddenly there's a flash of fur and growl of hot breath from what seems like every direction.

'There!' Peggy says, pointing off into the undergrowth. We creep after Peggy, away from the baying mob, but getting closer to werewolf Dylan.

'There she is!' I whisper. We walk between

two large trees and out from the shadows
comes Dylan, padding towards us with the
gait of a wild beast. The silhouette makes
me shudder with fright. Is it Dylan, is there
anything left of her in there, or has the moon's
power finally done its work? Her eyes are
glowing red in the darkness, like two laser
beams looking for prey. I can hear her rattling
breath, the steam from her nostrils fogging the
clear night sky. Does she even recognize me
any more? When she looks at me, does she
see me, her friend, or dinner? I don't have time
to think, or wait to find out. It's now or never.
We walk slowly towards her. I raise my hands.
'We mean you no harm Dylan,' I say slowly
and calmly. She looks at me, then at everyone,

then at Herbert dressed in his sausage suit and does a double take before letting out a hungry growl.

'Take off your trousers and feed them to Dylan.' I say to him. For a second he looks unsure then realizes that it's probably for the best. He whips them off and throws them down. Dylan wanders out into the moonlight. It's only then that I can see what a monster she has truly become. She is covered in thick

wiry hair, her teeth are huge and dripping with wolf dribble. She begins to chomp away on the meat. I turn on the phone app and point it at Dylan. There is her face on the screen. Every move I make is slow and deliberate, I don't want to antagonize her or scare her off. All I have to do is press the back arrows and the app will go into reverse. I'm just about to do it when someone grabs the phone from my hands.

'What are you doing, you don't have enough Happy Points for this!' Courtney screeches, snitching me to Pipper and Kipper who arrive just behind her. Then her eyes move to Dylan, 'Oh my, look at this!' she cries out. 'EVERYONE, I HAVE FOUND THE BEAST!'

'No, what are you doing?! Give me that phone back, I can fix this!' I shout.

'What, this phone?' she says looking at it. 'Too late, you are guilty of harbouring a werewolf!' she says, and without me being able to do a thing she throws the phone over her head, as far into the deep forest as she can. I hear a soft thud as it lands in the damp moss.

'NOOOOOOO!' I yell, 'you idiot, you've ruined everything, how am I supposed to fix Dylan now?'

'Dylan is gone, my word, look at her. She's a beast! She is the first recorded werewolf in history, and now she's mine. Surround her!' Courtney yells. 'I'll split the reward with everyone,' she calls out. 'Think of the fame it's going to bring me, all those TV requests. I'll probably write a song about it, and it'll probably win a Grammy,' Courtney smiles, her eyes lighting up. 'I'll stuff you and hang you on my wall. And oh my, I didn't even think about my bump in Instagram traffic. I'm hashtagging this as the best day ever!'

Slowly everyone surrounds Dylan. My

friend, they're going to kill my friend.

Dylan looks up from her meat feast of sausages and starts to claw away at the dirt, like a bull just before it charges. She hasn't taken her eye off Courtney's hand. The one that threw the phone away. Courtney begins to back away slowly.

'Good doggy,' she says. 'When I meant that I'll stuff you and hang you on the wall it was a figure of speech.' Courtney's face drains of all confidence along with all her colour too. 'Who's a good girl,' she says, voice trembling.

'Dylan, I can't help you if you do anything to Courtney,' I plead. But Dylan isn't listening to me, she's just staring at Courtney with a really intense look in her eyes. And then, like a jack-in-box, she leaps towards her, her teeth snarling and claws out. Courtney lets out a scream and closes her eyes, but Dylan leaps straight over her head and into the woods. There's a snarl and growl and a second later Dylan has returned with the phone in her mouth—she drops it at Courtney's feet and then jumps up and gives her a big lick on the face.

'Fetch, she's playing fetch,' Ashley says smiling.

'Ew, there's wolf drool all over me,' Courtney says, covered in slime.

SNAP comes the loud sound of a camera as Blane gets his phone out. 'That's a keeper,' he says, hitting 'Send'.

'Blane!' Courtney yells. 'Please tell me you didn't just tag me in that and post it.'

'Erm . . .'

'You and I are so finished. Again,' she snaps.

'Right! I'm having this phone before it causes any more damage,' Kipper says, marching over towards Courtney. But I reach out and grab it before he can get to it.

'No, wait, one more second,' I say hitting the app.

'No.'

'Please,' I say. Pointing the phone at Dylan I hit the back button and the phone begins to vibrate with power. 'Please work, please work,' I whisper.

'Give that to me!'

'Give Kipper the phone,' Pipper yells.

Just at that second the moon appears again from behind a cloud. It's huge and bright, it's the biggest moon I've ever seen. The phone starts to shake and fizz with electricity.

'It's too powerful!' I yell.

'Turn it off!' Ashley cries.

'I can't!'

BANG! The phone explodes into a thousand pieces, sending electrical pulses into the forest, like dancing spirits flying off never to be seen again. The light is blinding and everyone instinctively hits the ground.

The moon disappears once more and we are plunged into darkness.

Peggy is the first to her feet. She grabs a torch from the ground and fires it up.

'Dylan!' Ashley yells, searching the dark clearing for a sign of our friend.

Peggy points the torch at where Dylan was standing. There on the ground is a girl, not an animal, not a scary wolf, but a girl, my friend!

'What happened?' Dylan says, getting to her feet. 'I had a really weird dream, there were ears and a boy with sausage trousers . . .' she mumbles. Then suddenly she starts tapping the top of her head, like she's looking for something. 'Was I . . .? Was I a dog?!' she suddenly asks.

'Yes,' I say. 'It's my fault for bringing that stupid phone.' I shake my head sadly.

'I blame you too,' Ashley says, getting to her feet.

'I was messing with unstable technology, I didn't mean for anyone to get hurt.'

'Thanks for saving me,' Dylan smiles.

'It wasn't just us. We couldn't have done it

without these guys too. I guess Woodlice are good for something after all. If this was TV, I'd give you all a hug now,' Ashley says, looking over affectionately at Peggy, Herbert, and the rest of the gang. 'But it's not,' she says coldly.

'I'm lucky to have you guys!' Dylan giggles. 'Thanks for everything. Maybe this place isn't so bad after all.'

'I hate this place!' Courtney yells. 'Why couldn't you have let me slay you, Dylan? It's so selfish of you.'

'Sorry Courtney,' Dylan says, shyly.

'OK folks!' I yell out. 'Show's over, thanks for all your work, I'm sure we can arrange for you all to get your 'angry mob' badges, along with whittling and campfire management. But it's time to go back to your bunks now. I'm sure the next uprising is just around the corner.'

There's an audible sigh and a few huffs before the crowd begins to melt away.

'Hey, where did Pipper and Kipper go?' I ask.

'We're here! Is everyone all right?' Pipper says, getting unsteadily to her feet.

'Agh!' There's a gasp from Kipper as he gets to his feet too.

'What?' Pipper says, looking round, then another gasp. 'Kipper, you have ears, and . . . and . . .'

'A tail!' Kipper says pointing at Pipper. Sure enough, right in front of me are two camp leaders who are now giant squirrels.

'Oh great,' I say looking at the scorch marks on my hand where my phone once sat. 'OK, OK, I've fixed it once, I can fix it again. Who here has a tin of soup . . .'

'Or . . .' Kipper says.

'What?' I say.

'Yeah, what?' Ashley asks.

'Maybe . . .' Pipper says, 'we could just stay like this, you know for a bit. I really like your ears,' she says, smiling at Kipper.

'Ginger is a really good colour on you . . .' he says smiling at Pipper.

'So, you want to stay as giant squirrels?' I ask, just checking that we're all up to speed.

'Why not, it's certainly a selling point for the camp.'

'So when you talk about finding your inner animal, you literally meant it?' Ashley asks slowly.

'Yep.' They both grin at each other.

'Next summer,' I say, 'I am staying indoors with a book and absolutely no phones.'

ABOUT THE AUTHOR

Before becoming a writer and illustrator Tom spent nine years working as political cartoonist for *The Western Morning News* thinking up silly jokes about even sillier politicians. Then, in 2004 Tom took the plunge into illustrating and writing his own books. Since then he has written and illustrated picture books and fiction as well as working on animated TV shows for Disney and Cartoon Network.

Tom lives in Devon and his hobbies include drinking tea, looking out of the window, and biscuits. His hates include spiders and running out of tea and biscuits.

OTHER BOOKS BY
Tom McLaughlin

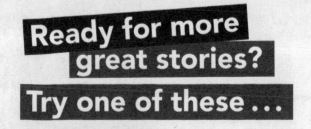

Ready for more great stories? Try one of these...